PRAISE FOR
CARLTON MELLICK III

"Easily the craziest, weirdest, strangest, funniest, most obscene writer in America."
—*GOTHIC MAGAZINE*

"Carlton Mellick III has the craziest book titles... and the kinkiest fans!"
—CHRISTOPHER MOORE, author of *The Stupidest Angel*

"If you haven't read Mellick you're not nearly perverse enough for the twenty first century."
—JACK KETCHUM, author of *The Girl Next Door*

"Carlton Mellick III is one of bizarro fiction's most talented practitioners, a virtuoso of the surreal, science fictional tale."
—CORY DOCTOROW, author of *Little Brother*

"Bizarre, twisted, and emotionally raw—Carlton Mellick's fiction is the literary equivalent of putting your brain in a blender."
—BRIAN KEENE, author of *The Rising*

"Carlton Mellick III exemplifies the intelligence and wit that lurks between its lurid covers. In a genre where crude titles are an art in themselves, Mellick is a true artist."
—*THE GUARDIAN*

"Just as Pop had Andy Warhol and Dada Tristan Tzara, the bizarro movement has its very own P. T. Barnum-type practitioner. He's the mutton-chopped author of such books as *Electric Jesus Corpse* and *The Menstruating Mall*, the illustrator, editor, and instructor of all things bizarro, and his name is Carlton Mellick III."
—*DETAILS MAGAZINE*

Also by
Carlton Mellick III

THE GIRL WITH THE BARBED WIRE HAIR

CARLTON MELLICK III

ERASERHEAD PRESS
PORTLAND, OREGON

ERASERHEAD PRESS
P.O. BOX 10065
PORTLAND, OR 97296

WWW.ERASERHEADPRESS.COM

ISBN: 978-1-62105-321-7

AUTHOR'S NOTE

When I was six years old, a strange man grabbed my hand while I was sleeping in my room at night and tried to pull me under the bed with him. My first thought when I woke up in a panic was that it was my older brother trying to mess with me, but my brother was fast asleep in his bed on the other side of the room. I was sure I was being attacked by something that wasn't human. As I struggled to get free, I prayed my brother would wake up to save me but I was too afraid to call out for help. Eventually I was able to wiggle my way out of the man's grip and leapt out of bed to turn the lights on. I woke up everyone in the house with my frantic shouting. But when my parents finally looked under the bed to see what the fuss was about, no one was there. The assailant just vanished. To this day, nobody believes me. Everyone is certain I just had a bad dream.

When I was twelve years old, I was home alone with my dog when there was banging coming from my sister's room. Just three loud knocks pounding on her bedroom wall. Because nobody was home, I had no idea who the hell it was. My dog started barking and growling in the hallway. Once the banging stopped, all of the paintings around me fell off of their nails and crashed on the floor. It freaked out my dog so much that he bit down on my leg as though I was the intruder. I had to pry open his jaw to get him to let go. Once we calmed down a little, I worked up the courage to get a butcher knife from the kitchen and open my sister's bedroom door to see who the hell was behind the noises. But no one was there. The only thing odd about her room was that all of the framed pictures had fallen off the walls and lay face down on her bed.

When I was in my twenties, I used to do writing marathons at a hotel that was known to be haunted. I thought it would be good for inspiration to write horror stories in a haunted hotel, but it turned out to be more of a nuisance than anything. I woke up several times to somebody grabbing my foot and shaking it as if trying to wake me up. I sometimes heard a young woman's voice whispering in my ear or singing a lullaby on the other side of the window. There was a time that I felt someone sit on the bed next to me and another time when I woke up with both of my arms and legs standing straight up in the air like something had erected them while I was unconscious and held them in place. I was especially freaked out by the time that I woke up with a woman's arms and legs wrapped around me. At first I thought I was at home with my girlfriend until it dawned on me that I was actually still in that haunted hotel room all by myself. I pulled myself out of the woman's grip and she rolled over. Before I could get a good look at who it was, she disappeared among the pile of sheets next to me and was gone.

All of these occurrences really unnerved me but I still returned to that hotel room for multiple writing marathons over the years. Every single visit was more extreme than the last, but I soldiered on and finished my work each and every time. But the final encounter was by far the most intense, so much that I thought it was going to kill me.

It was early morning on the last night of my writing marathon and the sun was just coming up. I was in the bed drifting in and out of sleep when I heard a young woman crying on the other side of the room near the closet. Because the morning light was pouring in from the window, I was clearly able to see some kind of shadowy figure with long hair standing about twelve feet away. But I really didn't want to know what it was so I didn't look for very long. I rolled over and faced the other direction, then I pulled the covers over my head like a scared little kid and hoped that I would just go back to sleep and not have to deal with anything supernatural.

When the crying stopped, my mind was able to rest and I felt myself falling back to sleep. But then I heard footsteps stomp across the floor as though the woman was charging at me. She jumped onto the bed and pierced me. I don't know how else to explain it. It was like she drove her hand right into my body. It felt like an electric shock pulsing through my entire nervous system. It was the most intense pain I'd ever felt in my life. And then it was like I was paralyzed. I tried to open my mouth to scream at the pain, but my lips wouldn't open, no sound would come out. At that moment I thought I was dead. I thought "This is it, I'm dying here."

The next thing I knew, I was being pulled out of my own body, like the crying woman had gripped onto my soul and was trying to tear it out. It was an odd sensation, like slipping out of a set of fleshy pajamas. I'd heard of people claiming to have out of body experiences before, but never expected it would happen to me, especially because I didn't believe in that kind of thing.

After she pulled me out of my skin, the woman crawled on top of me and looked me in the eyes. She wasn't exactly human. She was a black figure with skin that I could only describe as television static. Her hair covered my arms and chest. Because her back was to the window, blocking the light, I couldn't get a good look at her eyes staring at me through her long hair. But I could clearly see her television static lips as she leaned in and kissed me and slipped her tongue into my mouth. As she pulled my hand to her breast, I realized that she felt as real as a human. She wasn't made of energy like you'd expect. Her breasts were smaller and softer than any woman I'd ever been with, but they definitely were human.

I was terrified of what would happen if I rejected her, so I decided to just give in and go with it. I wasn't even sure if I was still alive as I felt the empty husk of my body lying next to me. As I realized I was making out with some kind of paranormal creature, I started to see the humor in the situation. I remember how my first thought was that I was glad that I wasn't overweight at the time. Years before, I was way too out of shape and doubt this ghost woman would have found me very attractive. But at that time I was in the best shape of my life. I was practically a ghost-chick-magnet. Of course she'd be all over me.

Honestly, though, it didn't seem like she wanted me because she found me attractive. She seemed lonely and desperate. The fact that she went from crying to attacking me to making love with me proved that she was an emotionally unbalanced spirit who was looking for something, anything to fill the hole that was inside her. It felt like she was just using me to feel alive again. Or at least that's what it seemed like to me.

I don't want to get into the gory details, but we did end up going all the way after that. The whole thing only lasted maybe ten minutes, but it was just as real as any sexual experience I've ever had. The girl climbed down from the bed and I fell back to sleep. I woke up a few hours later in my body, lying in the same position I was before I had been attacked. When I got home, I immediately told my girlfriend all about the experience and she seemed more excited about what had happened to me than I did. I guess having sex with a ghost wasn't technically cheating in her eyes.

Now after reading about these experiences I've had you're probably thinking that I'm either full of shit or completely insane and I don't blame you, but I promise that these stories are true. They were all very real events that I actually experienced. However, I'm even more skeptical about them than you are. Despite everything I went through, I don't actually believe in ghosts and never have. Even after having sex with one, I don't believe in the existence of any kind of paranormal phenomena. I'm pretty sure I was just suffering from sleep paralysis, which can cause a lot of strange but realistic-seeming experiences. Extreme stress can also cause hallucinations sometimes. Either way, I'm sure there's a reasonable explanation for everything that happened to me.

The Girl with the Barbed Wire Hair is the first ghost story of mine to ever see print. I've always loved reading ghosts stories, but I've never really had much of a desire to write one myself until now. Maybe because most ghost stories published these days fall under the label of "quiet horror" and I'm just not a "quiet horror" kind of a writer. Actually, I'm not really an *any* kind of horror person at all. I love reading it but I'll only write horror if I come up with a unique take on the genre, which is what I hope I've accomplished with this book.

So here it is, my 64th book. I hope you enjoy it!

—Carlton Mellick III 5/03/2022 7:06pm

PART ONE

CHAPTER
ONE

There is a girl who lives in the alley behind the old, abandoned fire station. She is always covered in ash and grime, cuts and bruises on her arms and legs, the skirt of her school uniform caked in dirt and ripped into tatters. Her hair is a mess of dreadlocks the color of rusted metal, growing like vines all the way down to her ankles.

Yusuke sees her on the way to school sometimes. She always keeps her distance, skittish like a wild animal. He often catches her peeking out of the broken windows of the firehouse or crossing his path like a stray cat. He wonders where she came from and why she is in such a sorry state. He assumes she must be a runaway, hiding so that she won't be taken back to an abusive household. Her home life must have been so bad that she'd rather live like this than return to her parents.

At first, Yusuke thought that he should maybe tell someone about the girl. He thought that the police should know about her living conditions, perhaps they'd be able to do something to help her. She seems to be about the same age as Yusuke and should be going to school like all the other kids. She obviously needs somebody to help her out. But knowing the police in this town, the incompetent self-important assholes who treat you like a nuisance whenever you call them for help, Yusuke knew it would only make the girl's situation worse. They would only send her right back to her abusive household and force her to endure the life she thought she escaped. So, Yusuke decided to leave her alone and let her live the way she wants to live.

Yusuke always feels sorry for the girl. He wishes he could do something for her, something to ease her suffering. That's why he started leaving gifts for her every day on the way to school. Right behind the old firehouse, he'd leave some piping hot melon bread on a paper plate, a basket of tomatoes his mom wanted to throw out, a fruit salad sandwich he made himself with strawberry, kiwi, banana, and heavy whipped cream wrapped in wax paper. He has left a cat puzzle and a Slinky and the first few volumes of *Ouran High School Host Club* so that she would have something to occupy her time while living on her own.

Whenever he returned to the alley on the way home from school, he would find the remains of the gifts he left for her—the crumbs from the melon bread scattered on the paper plate, the remains of mutilated tomatoes squished to the bottom of his mother's fruit basket, the crusts of the sandwich he made left on the cream-smeared wax paper. The puzzle was completely finished and displayed on the cracked asphalt trail, the slinky was dangling from a pile of bricks that had been carefully stacked into stairs, the books were ripped apart and scattered across the alleyway as though the girl only wanted to pull out some select illustrations that were trapped within.

The more items Yusuke leaves for her, the more frequently he would see her on his trips to school. It was as though she had become excited to see what he would bring her next, hoping that he would give her something delicious or fun to play with. He would catch glimpses of her peeking out of the bushes in the nearby forest, waiting for her next present. Yusuke was happy to give her gifts whenever he could. He didn't have any close friends at school and knowing that there was at least one person in town who was excited to see him brought him a sense of comfort. He wondered if he could be friends with this girl someday. He wondered if he could help her, maybe save her from her harsh and lonely lifestyle.

But when he actually comes in close contact with the girl for the first time, he wonders if she is somebody that he'd want to become friends with. She stands there in his path, staring at him with deep sunken eyes hidden in shadow, breathing hoarsely and drooling from cracked gray lips. Her long fingers are black and bloody like she's been trying to claw through asphalt. Her skin is pale and oily like she's spent all day bathing in a pool of grease. But the strangest thing about her is her hair. Instead of human hair growing out of her head, she has long strands of rusted barbed wire. He's not sure if the barbed wire is tangled within her actual hair or if somehow it has been implanted into her skull as some kind of punishment.

Either way, Yusuke can tell there's something seriously wrong with this girl. She is definitely not the person he thought she might be.

The sight of her makes Yusuke want to run away. She appears to be more animal than human. She seems like a rabid creature who will tear his throat out as soon as he opens his mouth to scream. But the girl doesn't stay for very long. She just looks at him for a moment and then runs away, disappearing into the woods without uttering a sound.

That night, Yusuke asks his mother about the girl who lives behind the old fire station. After he explains the appearance of the girl, his mother just stares blankly at him.

"You should stay far away from that girl," she tells him. "She's not somebody you want to deal with."

But this only interests Yusuke more.

"You know about her? Who is she?"

His mother pulls his steaming bowl of leftover curry out of the microwave oven and says, "Just stay away from her."

"But she's covered in cuts and bruises. There's all this barbed wire tangled in her hair. I think she needs help."

His mother's tone becomes aggressive. "She doesn't need anyone's help. Don't go near her ever again."

Then she places the steaming plate of food in front

of him and locks herself in her bedroom for the rest of the night. Yusuke has no idea what's gotten into her or why she wouldn't explain to him what she knows. Perhaps everyone knows about the girl and thinks it's best to just leave her the way she is. Perhaps she's just someone that everyone thinks would be best left forgotten.

Yusuke doesn't bring the girl any presents on the way to school today. He considers taking a different route, maybe going down Main Street like the other kids do. But that path is so long that it would take him an extra half hour to make it to class. He's always been late whenever he's gone that way. He doesn't want to get into trouble again.

After hesitating for a few minutes at the mouth of the path, he decides to make a dash for it. He runs down the alleyway, keeping his eyes on the walkway ahead, ready to pull back if the strange girl appears ahead of him.

He moves so quickly that he doesn't see her until it's too late. He trips on something and crashes into the pavement. At first, he thinks he stumbled over a pile of garbage until he notices her feet beneath him. Muddy toes and black toenails extrude from her tattered shoes inches from his face. The girl kicks and squirms beneath him.

When Yusuke gets to his feet and backs away, he sees the girl on the ground. Her barbed wire hair is tangled in the fence surrounding the old firehouse. It's wrapped around her wrists and waist, trapping her in place. She thrashes and struggles, but can't get herself free. Her deep sunken eyes are locked onto his. Shivering and grinding her teeth, a screeching noise bubbles from her throat that sounds like a cross between whimpering and growling. She seems terrified.

But Yusuke is far more afraid of her than she is of him. One look into her cold catlike eyes, and he runs away. He jumps over her legs and rushes out of the alleyway to safety.

When Yusuke exits the alleyway, he's moving so fast that he crashes into Narumi Wada, the most popular girl in junior high. He knocks her books out of her hands and they scatter across the sidewalk. When he sees the look of shock and anger on her face, he bows at her three times and says, "I'm sorry. I'm so sorry."

"Why don't you look where you're going?" Narumi yells at him.

"I'm so sorry!"

Yusuke picks up her books and hands them to her. Narumi's not the kind of girl you want to piss off. Even though she's the most beautiful girl in school, she has a reputation for being an awful bitch who will make your life a living hell if you get on her bad side. One word to any of the many boys who are in love with her and you'll find an army of bullies determined to make you pay for your mistreatment of her for the rest of the school year.

But as Yusuke hands over her textbooks, Narumi doesn't seem as angry as he expected she would be. The expression on her face is one of curiosity more than anything.

"Did you just come out of the alley?" she asks him.

Yusuke looks back at where he came from and then nods his head, still trying to catch his breath. "Yeah."

Her eyes light up. "Did you see her?"

Yusuke is confused. He wonders if she's talking about who he thinks she's talking about.

"See who?" he asks.

"The girl with the barbed wire hair," Narumi says.

Yusuke pauses when she says this, shocked that she would bring the feral girl up so casually. He wonders if he misheard her. Maybe she's talking about somebody else and his mind went straight to the girl he just saw in the alleyway. But when he looks Narumi Wada in her glossy eyes, her eyebrows raised with anticipation, he can tell she's being straight with him.

"You know about her?" Yusuke asks.

"Of course I do. Everyone knows about her!"

Yusuke points behind him. "I saw her just now. That's what I was running from."

"Holy shit!" The girl smiles even wider, looking back at the alleyway. "Are you serious? I've never known anyone who's seen her before."

"I tripped over her. She nearly scared me to death."

"That's so crazy! I used to go in the alley when I was a kid but I was never able to see her. What did she look like?"

Yusuke shrugs. "Kind of like a wild animal."

"She didn't try to attack you or anything?" Narumi asks, moving closer to him. "They say she attacks anyone who enters her territory."

Yusuke gets a little uncomfortable with how close she's getting to him. He's never spoken to Narumi before, he's never gotten a good look at her up close. But he now understands why people think she's the most beautiful girl in school. She has big black eyes that illuminate your reflection. She has long black hair that's straightened perfectly, with symmetrical bangs that end just before her large manicured eyebrows. He feels like he's melting just by being surrounded by her warm radiance.

Yusuke shakes his head. "No, she usually runs away from me whenever I see her."

"You have to tell me all about her. I've always been fascinated by that urban legend. I always hoped it was real."

Yusuke smiles and nods his head. "Sure. I'll tell you anything you want to know."

Narumi straightens her uniform and they walk to school together.

She tells him, "A lot of kids have gone missing by going through that alleyway. I'm surprised you have the guts to do that every day."

"It's the only way I can get to school on time," Yusuke says.

"You must be braver than you look," she says. "All

the other guys in school would shit their pants if they saw her even from a distance. Not even members of the judo club would go that way to school."

"I never thought she was dangerous. I always thought she looked kind of sad."

Yusuke decides to tell her the whole story, about how he leaves gifts for her every day, how she eats the food he gives her, plays with the toys, and rips up the books. He tells her about how he's seen her up close and how he tripped on her this morning while she was tangled up in the wire fence. His story makes Narumi laugh in delight. It's like he's become the most interesting guy in the world to the most beautiful girl in the school. He can't help but feel special.

Narumi changes the subject. "You're new this year, aren't you?"

Yusuke nods. "We moved in over the summer, but my parents grew up here. They inherited my grandmother's house after she died."

"That must be why you didn't know better than taking the alleyway to school. You didn't know that it's haunted."

"Haunted? You think the girl's a ghost?"

"Of course she's a ghost."

"She doesn't look like a ghost to me. Besides her disheveled looks and barbed wire hair, she's as human as you or me. I think she's just homeless and mentally ill."

Narumi laughs. "She's been haunting that alley for decades, even when my parents were kids. She's definitely a ghost."

Yusuke goes quiet for a while. He doesn't know what to believe. He doesn't think it's possible that the girl in the alley isn't alive. She ate the food he left her. He felt the warmth of her body when he fell on her. There's no way she's a ghost.

When they arrive at school, all the guys who hang out on the front steps give Yusuke dirty looks for walking alongside the prettiest girl in school. They glare at him with intense jealousy, especially when she hugs Yusuke goodbye and asks to meet him again after school. They look like they're planning to kick his ass the second Narumi leaves their sight, but Yusuke rushes to class before they have a chance to confront him.

After school, Narumi chases Yusuke down to talk to him some more. She seems rather angry that the unpopular shy kid didn't wait for her at the front entrance like any of the other guys would have.

"Wait up," Narumi calls out, running barefoot with her shoes over her shoulder. "I said wait!"

Yusuke stops and waits for her to catch up, looking back at the attractive girl with her hair blowing in the wind, her books sliding out of her hands, her skirt hiked up past her knees. When she arrives, Narumi catches her breath and leans on his shoulder so that she can put her shoes on her feet.

"Are you going to cut through the alleyway again?" Narumi asks.

Yusuke shakes his head. "I'll just take the long way home today."

Her eyes become annoyed. "What? I thought you walked that way every day. You're going to wimp out now?"

Yusuke shrugs. "She's probably still there, tied to the fence. I'd rather not see her if I don't need to."

"Come on, I thought you were cool." She moves ahead of Yusuke and leads the way. "I want to come with you. I want to see her myself."

Yusuke follows her. "Seriously? Even though you think she's a ghost?"

"I've been waiting years to find out if the stories are true," she says. "If you're not lying and actually have seen the girl, I want to see her too."

Yusuke thinks about it for a moment. He doesn't want to see the girl with the barbed wire hair again, but he wants to go if Narumi wants to go. Even if it's scary at least he'll be able to spend more time with the prettiest girl in school. At least it'll make her happy.

"Alright, we can go," Yusuke says.

"Great!" Narumi says, wrapping her arms around his. "I can't wait!"

Yusuke feels weird walking hand in hand with the prettiest girl in school. He knows she's not doing it because she likes him. It's almost like she's bullying him or at least manipulating him into doing whatever she wants him to do. But he doesn't mind either way.

"I hope she's terrifying!" Narumi cries.

A group of guys from school see Yusuke walking with Narumi wrapped around his arm and speed up to confront the two. As Yusuke hears their footsteps stomping in his direction, he looks back to see Hiroto and his two friends, Itachi and Touma. The three of them are the biggest, meanest kids in school, the ones who always carry box cutters around with them everywhere they go like weapons and claim to be from major yakuza families even though they lived their whole lives in a rural backwoods town. They smoke cigarettes on the roof of the art building and challenge other boys to fight whenever they can.

Nobody ever wants to become the target of Hiroto and his gang. It's basically a death sentence for the rest of your school life. And the worst part is that all of them are desperately in love with Narumi. Most people won't even talk to her out of fear of what they might do to them. Yusuke knows he's in trouble the second they laid eyes on them together. He lowers his head and trembles in a panic. Narumi can probably feel him shaking in her arm, but he can't help himself.

"What the fuck do you think you're doing, Zombie-chan?" Hiroto says.

Zombie-chan was Yusuke's nickname when he first moved to town. When they first met him, everyone thought he looked like the living dead the way he slowly roamed the halls with a dead expression on his face and never spoke to anyone. Yusuke is surprised Hiroto even knows about the name because he hasn't been referred to by it since his first month in school. Not only that, but they're not in any of the same classes and they've never interacted with each other before.

Yusuke wants to just keep walking, but Narumi turns around and smiles at the three boys. She's not the kind of person who would ever avoid confrontation, no matter how unpleasant. She's the complete opposite of Yusuke in every way.

"Hey, Big Bear, how's it going?" she says to him.

Hiroto hesitates from confronting her with anger since he obviously wants more than anything for her to like him. It disarms him a little.

"We're headed to the arcade," he says. "What are you doing hanging out with the walking dead?"

Narumi hugs Yusuke's arm tighter and says, "He's my new pet. Are you jealous?"

Hiroto spits and says, "No. Why would I be jealous of Zombie Boy?" Even though it's completely obvious that he's fuming with jealousy.

As Hiroto and Narumi talk, the other two guys throw small pebbles at the back of Yusuke's head, trying their best not to hit the girl next to him. They giggle with each throw that hits. Yusuke brushes the pebbles out of his hair but otherwise tolerates them.

"He says he's seen the girl with the barbed wire hair," Narumi says. "We're going to try to find her."

Hiroto's eyes widen when she says this and he loses a breath. He stutters when he responds, "Bullshit. He's not man enough to take that alleyway."

Narumi snickers. "He walks this way to school every single day. He says he sees her all the time."

"Yeah right. He's lying."

Itachi adds, "There's no way he's seen her for real."

Narumi shrugs. "Maybe he is, maybe he isn't."

Itachi throws another pebble and pegs Yusuke right in the forehead. Yusuke stumbles back, more in shock than hurt by being hit in the face. Narumi rubs his forehead like a concerned mother and whispers to him, "Ahhh, poor thing. Don't worry about them."

This only annoys the boys more, but they stop throwing pebbles at him. They don't want to be responsible for giving the pretty girl a reason to show him anymore attention, even if she's doing it more in a demeaning way than an affectionate one.

"Want to come with us?" Narumi asks.

A devilish smile crosses her face. She knows Hiroto doesn't have the guts to agree.

"Fuck no," he tells them. "Why would I want to do that?"

"Suit yourself," Narumi says.

She turns Yusuke around and they continue on their way, heading in the direction of the alleyway.

The three boys follow after them.

As they walk, Hiroto comes up alongside Yusuke and says, "I know you're full of shit, Zombie-chan. If you really saw the girl in the alleyway you'd be dead by now. You know she kills anyone she sees, don't you? If you go that way you're going to die."

His threats don't faze Yusuke. Even though they are meant to terrify him and make him too afraid to continue,

Yusuke has already seen the girl with the barbed wire hair. He thinks she's scary but she's never tried to hurt him. He doesn't even think she's a ghost. He thinks that's all just a misunderstanding.

Hiroto continues, "Everyone who's ever taken that path to school is never seen again. Not alive anyway. Do you really have the guts to risk that?"

It's obvious to Yusuke that the tough guy is trying to get him to wimp out so that he'll look stupid in front of Narumi. Since he isn't brave enough to go with them, his only choice is to deter them so that he doesn't look like the only coward.

"Think about how sad it will be for your mother once you turn up dead," Hiroto says. "Do you really want her to go through all that? It'll ruin her life. And if you have siblings she's going to take it out on them. She's going to blame them for surviving when their other child is gone. You don't want that to happen, do you?"

The bullies continue to harass and dissuade them from continuing with their plans, but once Narumi and Yusuke step one foot on the path leading down the alleyway, the three of them stop in their tracks and won't go any farther.

"Sure you don't want to come with us?" Narumi asks them.

Hiroto thinks about it for a second. He's shaking and beginning to sweat. But there's a look of terror on his face. He can't get himself to agree and can't even think of a good reason to refuse without coming across as a coward.

"Come on, let's just go," Touma tells Hiroto.

"Yeah," Itachi says, "if the zombie kid saw her and lived we'll be fine. And if she does attack we can just push him down so that she'll go after him and we can get away."

Hiroto gives them a dirty look. Then he says, "Fuck this. We've got better things to do."

As they turn to walk away, Hiroto says loud enough for Yusuke to hear, "If he really did see her she probably thought he was already dead and didn't bother killing him. That's the only way he'd survive."

They walk away, trying to still act cool despite visibly trembling in a panic.

Hiroto yells out, "You better not die, Narumi. You still owe me a date like you promised."

Narumi yells back, "Yeah, yeah. Whatever you say, Scaredy-kun."

And walks deeper into the alley with Yusuke.

"Don't worry about him, Zombie-chan," Narumi says as they stroll down the alleyway. "You're twice the man he is if you're willing to face the girl with barbed wire hair. No guy in school has the guts to seek her out except for you."

Yusuke nods. He doesn't see himself as brave, but he is confused about how afraid the other guys were. They didn't seem like the kind who would be afraid of anything.

"Why is everyone so scared of her?" he asks.

"They all heard the stories," Narumi says. "Hiroto is especially scared of the girl because she killed his older brother five years ago."

"Are you serious?"

Narumi nods. "He was dared to take the alleyway on the way home from school back when he was in junior high. Since he was known to be the toughest, bravest kid he did it without hesitation. But he never came out the other side. Nobody saw him ever again."

"He just disappeared?"

"Nobody found the body, but everyone knows the girl with barbed wire hair got him. She probably ripped him apart into pieces so small that there wasn't a body left for them to find."

Yusuke looks away, scanning the path ahead of them. He believes Narumi is telling the truth but wonders if what she thinks is what really happened. Maybe Hiroto's brother just ran away or was kidnapped or got himself killed in some other way. He doesn't want to know what will happen if the stories about the girl with the barbed wire hair are true.

"There are a lot of stories like that, though," Narumi continues. "Two kids disappeared just last year. Three a couple years before that. I don't know how many died total, but there's been dozens of unexplained deaths and disappearances from our school over the years. When I was a kid, I saw a girl hanging from a tree at the entrance of the alleyway. All the kids came out to see it once the police arrived. They say it was suicide, but she was hung with barbed wire wrapped around her neck. Who would kill themselves with barbed wire? And the look on her face was one of horror, like she died screaming and struggling. The palms of her hands were all cut up from trying to climb the wire like a rope. There's no way that was suicide. I knew it had to be the ghost who killed her."

Yusuke listens intently. She doesn't seem to be joking around with him. She's definitely the kind of girl who likes to lie and manipulate people for fun, but her tone of voice is one of complete honesty. He doubts she would be here if it was just to tell him about the local ghost stories, but it does make him wonder why she would be going with him if she believed these horrific events really happened.

"That's what got me so obsessed with the girl in the alleyway," Narumi explains. "I wanted so bad for it to be real. It would be so cool if there really was a ghost haunting our town and killing kids that go to our school."

"Aren't you scared, though?" Yusuke asks.

Narumi nods. "I'm a huge fan of horror movies. I like being scared."

Then she squeezes Yusuke's arm against her ribs, the tie of her school uniform draped over his wrist.

"I hope she'll still be tangled up when we get there," Narumi says. "I can't wait to see her for real."

Yusuke nods. He's definitely not excited to see the strange girl again, but he does hope she'll be there if it will make Narumi happy. He doesn't know what will happen if the feral girl has pulled herself free when they arrive. He wonders if they will be attacked and killed. He wonders if Narumi will be terrified or excited. But as scary as that idea sounds, Yusuke thinks it might also be bad if the girl isn't there at all anymore. If they don't come across her Narumi will probably be mad. He kind of likes that an attractive girl is showing him so much attention and doesn't want her to hate him after this.

Almost as though she was reading his mind, Narumi says, "By the way, I'm going to be so pissed if you were lying to me and she's not where you said she was." Her tone changed to that of a vengeful bitch. "I'm going to tell everyone at school you tried to rape me if this is all bullshit. You're going to get your ass kicked or arrested or worse."

And with those words, Yusuke tenses up and fills with panic. He prays the ghost girl is still where he left her, even if it kills them both.

CHAPTER
TWO

Ever since he was a little kid, Yusuke was obsessed with the idea of the supernatural. He loved the idea of ghosts and spirits and beings from other worlds. He especially liked the women from folklore with mystical powers and wisdom beyond their years. Like the nine-tailed fox in female form, or the dullahan with a missing head, or the Yuki-onna snow spirit who was made of ice and froze men's hearts.

Yusuke used to buy or make figurines of his favorite ghost women from Greek, Celtic, and Japanese folklore. He had several of them lining the shelves. Other guys in school might have been obsessed with magical girls and cat girls and battle maids from their favorite anime, but Yusuke liked women with paranormal characteristics. He liked them to be ethereal and ancient and have the ability to walk through walls or appear before you whenever you had pleasant thoughts about them.

He always thought about how amazing it would be if he fell in love with them like many of the men did in the old folktales. Having a nine-tailed fox for a girlfriend sounded so enchanting. Kissing a girl who pulled him into a mirror world all their own sounded like a fantasy that he'd love to come true. But unlike Narumi, Yusuke has always hated horror movies. He doesn't like being scared. He would never be interested in the grotesque monstrous ghost women in old horror movies like Sadako from *Ringu* and Kayako from *Ju-On*. They were so gross and terrifying. They're not at all the kind of paranormal creatures that Yusuke is interested in.

If the girl in the alley behind the old fire station is a ghost, then she'd be nothing like Yusuke was looking for in a supernatural woman. She doesn't have the ages-old wisdom of a nine-tailed fox or the beauty of the Yuki-onna. She's just a lost feral kid with the mentality of a wild animal. She's more like a monster than a mystical spirit.

When Yusuke and Narumi come across the girl in the alleyway, both of them recoil in disgust. She's still tangled up in her barbed wire hair and bound to the chain link fence behind her. It's only gotten worse, though. Her arms and legs are sliced up, her uniform ripped open, exposing the middle portion of her small sweat-stained bra. She's been struggling all day but still can't free herself.

"Holy shit," Narumi cries. "She's real! I can't believe she's really real!"

Narumi lets go of Yusuke's arm and steps closer, but not too close. She's shivering a little, acting slightly cautious as she moves in for a better look.

"But she looks kind of pathetic, doesn't she?" Narumi says. "I thought she'd be a lot scarier."

Yusuke nods. "I don't think she's a ghost. I think she's a real person."

Narumi ignores him and picks up a stick from a nearby tree. She goes to the tangled girl and pokes at her. The girl with barbed wire hair screeches and hisses, unable to do anything about being prodded with a stick. Her deep black eyes are filled with embarrassment and anguish.

"She's so fucked up," Narumi says. "Look at her face."

This is the first time Yusuke's been able to really get a good look at the feral girl. She can't move, she's not able to run away from him, and he's not running away from her. He's now able to see how innocent she looks. She has sad eyes, the eyes of a lonely girl who doesn't have any friends. Yusuke has seen those eyes many times before. He's seen them every time he looks at himself in the mirror, ever since he was ostracized by his friends back in middle school. The more he looks at her, the less scary she becomes. She's like Narumi describes her—pathetic and pitiable.

"Actually, she's kind of pretty," Narumi says, examining her more carefully. "Do you think she's pretty?"

Yusuke never thought of her as pretty or ugly before, but when he thinks about it he can see what Narumi means.

"Yeah, a little," Yusuke says.

"I bet she was super cute before she died," Narumi

says. "If you clean her up and get rid of all the barbed wire, I bet a lot of guys would be into her."

Yusuke just nods.

Narumi squats down in front of the tangled girl, right between her legs. She looks her right in the eyes and says, "Are you really the ferocious killer I thought you were? You don't look like you'd be capable of killing all those missing kids."

"Are you sure it's not just a coincidence?" Yusuke asks. "Maybe somebody took her out of an insane asylum, implanted barbed wire in her hair, and dropped her off in this alleyway just to make people believe the urban legend was real."

Narumi shrugs and backs away. "I don't know who the hell would go through all that trouble, but maybe."

"She really doesn't seem like a ghost to me," Yusuke says. "She just seems like a sad lost girl who lives in the alleyway. She even got herself tangled up in the fence. What kind of ghost would do that?"

Narumi lets out a long breath of air. "Hmmm. Yeah, maybe you're right." She tosses her stick into the woods. "I'm kind of bored with her. Let's just get out of here."

"Really?" Yusuke asks. "Shouldn't we try to get her free?"

Narumi shrugs. "Go ahead if you want to. Whether she's a ghost or just a random crazy chick, she'll probably rip your throat out the second you get her free. I'd just leave her alone if I were you."

Yusuke nods and follows her out of the alley.

"Well, that was pretty fucked up to see," Narumi says,

a smile spreading across her face. "A little disappointing, but still kind of fun. I wonder if all the legends are a hoax after all."

"At least you got to see her with your own eyes," Yusuke says.

"Yeah, I guess," Narumi says, looking down at the books in her hands. "But it would've been more fun if she tried to kill us."

"You think that would be fun?"

The corner of her lips curls into a half-smile. "Yeah. I mean, it would suck if she hurt or killed me, but I was hoping she would at least murder you." She laughs when she sees the horrified look on Yusuke's face. "I'm sure I could outrun you. It would have been so cool to see her tackle you to the ground, tangle you up in her barbed wire hair and rip you up limb from limb. It would have been like seeing a gruesome horror movie in real life."

Yusuke can't believe she actually said that, but assumes she must just be messing with him, just to get a rise out of him. He decides to go along with it. "Well, sorry you didn't get to see me die."

As they get to the end of the alleyway, Narumi bursts into laughter. "You know, you're not such a bad guy, Zombie-chan. I kind of like you."

Her words make Yusuke blush. He knows she doesn't *really* like him, but any kind of compliment from a girl as beautiful as Narumi makes him happy.

"You should speak up more in class," Narumi says. "People would like you if they knew what a badass you are."

"I'm not a badass…" Yusuke says.

"Sure you are," she tells him. "Do you know how many other guys in school would have actually come with me into that alleyway? None of them. Just you. As far as I'm concerned, you're the coolest guy in school."

Then without warning, she kisses him on the cheek.

"Thanks for showing me a good time," she tells him. "See you around."

And the next thing Yusuke knows, she's waving goodbye and walking away, heading in the direction of her home. Yusuke doesn't even have a chance to wave back before she crosses the street and disappears from his sight.

When Yusuke gets home, he feels like he's on cloud nine. He can't believe he was kissed by the prettiest girl in school, even if it was only a peck on the cheek. He never even thought much of Narumi. She's so far out of his league that he never even thought himself worthy of looking at her before today. He's not one of the boys who worship at the Church of Narumi like so many others in his class. Even if it was just under an hour, it was still more than most of the other guys have ever spent with her. If word spreads around, he's going to be either the most popular or the most despised boy in school tomorrow. It might even be worth all the serious bullying he's going to receive from Hiroto and his friends once they finally get a hold of him.

But once Yusuke stops thinking about Narumi's kiss on his cheek, he remembers the look of anguish on the girl they left in the alleyway. They just left her there, wrapped up in barbed wire and tied to the chain link fence. He doesn't like the idea of her being stuck there overnight. Even if she's mentally ill, even if she's the tormented ghost from local folklore, he doesn't like the idea of her being stuck in that position. She could die if nobody does something. And the fact that everyone avoids that area of town, he knows nobody's ever going to find her if she is unable to free herself.

Yusuke can't stop the guilt from overwhelming his brain. He tries to do homework. He tries to play his new Hidetaka Miyazaki video game. But he just can't get his mind off of that sad, helpless girl behind the old fire station.

Before he knows what he's doing, Yusuke goes into the basement and locates his dad's wire cutters from a toolbox. Then he leaves the house and heads back to the place where they left the girl with the barbed wire hair.

The sun is starting to go down, but Yusuke is determined to get the job done. He doesn't like the idea of being alone in the dark with the feral girl but his conscience won't allow him to give up and return home. He moves quickly, hoping to get it done as soon as he possibly can.

When he arrives at the girl in the back alleyway, she

doesn't seem very pleased to see him. She thrashes and gnashes her teeth at him, desperate to break out of her bonds and attack him for coming so close. She's even more ferocious than when she was with Narumi, knowing that he's not someone to be trusted, not the guy who brought the girl who poked at her with a stick and said horrible things about her. But Yusuke is determined to set her free.

"Don't worry, I just want to help," Yusuke says.

He brings the wire cutters toward her and she lashes out at him, striking with her less-tethered arm even though it's still not enough to reach him. Yusuke tries to act as unthreatening as he can, lifting up the wire cutters to show that they're not something she should be worried about.

"I'm just trying to set you free," he says.

She struggles more fiercely than ever as he grabs hold of one of the strands of barbed wire tangled in the chain link fence. She growls and hisses as he brings the wire cutters closer and snips it off at the knot.

The girl cries out when the wire is cut, as though it is part of her nervous system. She kicks and writhes, screaming at him like a banshee. But Yusuke is determined to get the job done. He moves on to the next wire pinning her in place and cuts it as quickly as he can. The girl screams loudly, howling at the darkening sky.

"I'm sorry," he tells her. "I know it hurts, but it's the only way to get you free."

Yusuke is worried about what's going to happen once she's liberated enough to reach him with her long black fingernails. He's worried that she will strike without mercy, cut gashes into his arms and face. But he proceeds anyway. He's hoping he can get her loose before she has the chance to attack him.

"It's okay…" Yusuke says, trying to soothe her, getting her to relax.

He rubs her shoulder, showing her that he means no harm. Her skin is bare where he touches her, in a section of her uniform that has been ripped away. She's strangely warm, warmer than somebody would be who's been sitting in the cold all day, warmer than any ghost Yusuke's ever heard of before. He's surprised that she reacts well to his touch. She calms down quite a bit and allows him to cut more of her barbed wire hair without lashing out at him. He pets her like a stray dog whose leash got tangled around a mailbox.

Yusuke looks over at her and notices that she's staring into him with her deep black eyes. She's almost crying as she looks at him, as though she now understands that he's only trying to help her, as though nobody's ever shown her any kind of human kindness in her entire life. Her gray lips tremble, maybe trying to tell him how much she appreciates what he's doing for her.

With every cut of the barbed wire, the girl no longer reacts with anger, she no longer cries out in pain. She still cringes with each snap of the wire cutters, but Yusuke realizes it's only because of the vibrations against her scalp whenever he cuts through a strand of her metal hair. All he has to do is hold the wire steady when he squeezes the wire cutters and it won't hurt her so much.

When Yusuke finishes cutting through all the barbed wire that was holding the girl in place, he backs away. The girl shakes her hair and gets to her feet, but she doesn't run away nor attack him. She just looks at him with wet black eyes and trembling lips.

"There you go," Yusuke tells her. "You're free now."

She steps closer to him, as though she wants to thank him, maybe even hug him, but he doesn't let her come too close to him. The sun is no longer in the sky and it's almost dark. He doesn't want to stick around for much longer. He can't imagine how scary it will be once the sky is completely black. There aren't any street lights on this side of town. He'd be with her in total darkness.

"Try to be more careful," he tells her. "I don't want to have to cut you free again."

The girl looks a lot different with her barbed wire hair cut short. She almost looks like a normal girl, standing there in her school uniform, shivering in the cold. She reaches out her arms for comfort.

Yusuke turns to leave, moving quickly to get out of there as soon as possible. He assumes the girl will run away at any second, but she doesn't flee. Instead, she follows him through the alleyway. When he turns back, she stops. Her lips are still trembling, her eyes still watery with gratitude.

"It's no big deal," Yusuke says. "I just didn't want you to be stuck like that all night."

She inches closer. It's as though she wants to hug him, show him love and appreciation. But Yusuke has no intention of getting that close to her. He turns and picks up his pace, trying to get out of the alley as quickly as he can. The girl keeps following him, all the way to the other side of the alley. He's worried that she won't let him leave. He's worried that she'll be offended and attack at any second.

But nothing happens. Yusuke leaves the alleyway and goes toward the main street just before nightfall. He looks back at every other block, wondering if the girl is still following. There's a shadowy figure hiding behind the buildings at every cross street, but he can't tell if it's her or just his imagination. He hopes it's just in his head. He doesn't know what he'd do if the girl with the barbed wire hair was able to pursue him beyond the limits of the alleyway behind the old fire station.

When Yusuke gets home, his mother reprimands him for being late.

"What are you doing out past dark?" she asks him. "You'll get behind in your subjects."

She's sitting on the living room floor, going through a week's worth of mail on the coffee table and drinking Nigori cream sake.

"I'm sorry, mom," he says. "I needed to help out a friend."

"You don't need friends. You need to get into a good high school so that you can get into a good college."

"She's not really a friend. Just somebody I know that needed help."

"A student's job is to study," his mother says.

"I know, mom."

"Go up to your room and get your work done. I'll have dinner ready when you're finished."

Yusuke nods and goes upstairs. Because he doesn't have any kind of social life and isn't allowed to waste time on video games or watching anime, Yusuke has always been a good student and has never had problems getting all of his work done. He's usually farther ahead in his studies than any of his classmates even though he's far from the smartest kid in class. His mother has no reason to worry about him falling behind.

After an hour of school work, Yusuke is already free to waste time reading manga and decorating his figurine collection. He grabs a copy of the new volume of *Black Renegade* and drops down on his bed, propping up his feet on the windowsill.

Black Renegade is his favorite manga right now. It's about an immortal half-demon female samurai who hunts down evil demonic creatures that are lured to her whenever she menstruates. Yusuke loves characters like the *Black Renegade* because she's a realist and strategic-thinker and doesn't care to deal with overly sensitive idealist types who act with their hearts instead of their brains. She's actually the kind of person he wishes he could be, especially if he was transported to a strange fantasy world.

As Yusuke flips through the pages of the manga, he sees something out the window that catches his eye. A shadowy figure is lingering on the street below, peeking out from behind the burned-out street lamp in front of his home. Yusuke's first thought is that it's a neighbor waiting for a ride or smoking a cigarette, but then he notices that the person is staring right into his window, staring right at him. When he sees the barbed wire curling around the lamppost, Yusuke freezes and drops the book from his hands.

The girl with the barbed wire hair had followed him home. She's out there like some kind of creepy stalker, watching him as he reads and does his homework. When their eyes meet, the girl steps out from behind the post, as though moving toward him. She inches all the way to the steps leading up to his house and then pauses, looking up at him like she wants something from him, like a stray cat wanting to be fed. She opens her mouth as though she wants to call out to him, but she doesn't speak. She lifts her hand from her waist as though she's about to wave, but doesn't do anything but stretch out her fingers before hiding her hands beneath the remaining strands of her barbed wire hair.

Yusuke jumps to his feet and pulls the curtains shut, then steps away from the window. He has no idea why she followed him home or what she could possibly want with him. He didn't even think she was able to leave the alleyway behind the old fire house. If she's a ghost, she should be trapped in the area where she originally died. Unless she really isn't a ghost just as Yusuke first assumed.

Yusuke can't stop trembling as he goes downstairs to eat dinner. He doesn't feel safe with the girl lingering outside. While sitting down at the dinner table, eating the cold soba noodle salad his mother left for him, he watches the front door, keeps a close eye on all the windows on the ground level, terrified that the girl might try to break in.

His mother comes downstairs and asks him if he's done his homework. Yusuke just nods and twirls soba noodles around his chopsticks, keeping his eyes on the front door.

"Your father's business trip got extended so he won't be home until next week," his mother says.

Yusuke just nods.

"He says he wants you to wash his car and vacuum the interior before he gets back. He has to entertain a client the night he gets back so it needs to be spotless, as clean as a rental."

Yusuke agrees without fully listening to what she's asked of him. She continues to list off other tasks she wants him to do while his father is away, but he's too focused on the front door to hear what she's saying. He can't tell with the volume of his mother's voice but he swears that he hears a scratching noise coming from the front door. It's like the feral girl is scraping into the wood with her long black fingernails, trying to dig her way through the door.

Once Yusuke decides that it must be his imagination,

48

his mother stops talking and reacts to the noise. She goes quiet and turns around, listening for where the scratching is coming from.

"What is that sound?" she asks.

The noise gets louder. Yusuke is sure it's the feral girl now. She's scratching at the door as though she wants somebody to let her in.

His mother goes in the direction of the front door and says, "Must be that damn neighbor's cat."

She reaches out her hand to open the door, planning to shush the feline away. But before she can, Yusuke yells out, "Don't open the door!"

His mother hesitates, pausing as her hand rests on the door handle.

"What? Why?" she asks.

Yusuke stutters. He doesn't have a good excuse. He'd rather not tell her about the girl with the barbed wire hair, but he doesn't want her to open the door either. He doesn't know what would happen if the feral girl got inside.

"It might not be a cat," he says. But he doesn't explain further. It's the best he could come up with on the spot.

"Then what is it?" his mother asks.

But before Yusuke has to answer, the scratching stops. Whatever it was has gone away. His mother listens carefully, but there's nothing left to investigate. She opens the door, against Yusuke's protests, but there's nothing there.

"Must have run away," she says.

Then she closes the door and locks it. Yusuke takes

a deep breath of relief and goes back to eating. He has no idea what would've happened if the girl had gotten inside. She might have killed them both, ripped them into pieces like what happened to Hiroto's older brother. Yusuke couldn't handle the thought of being responsible for his mother's death. Even if he didn't do it with his own hands, leading a psychotic killer home is enough for him to blame himself for whatever would have happened next. He's thankful they are both safe. He just hopes they remain safe until the feral girl finally decides to move on.

When he goes upstairs, Yusuke looks out the window, searching for any sign of the feral girl. But she's nowhere to be seen. She's no longer by the lamppost, she's nowhere near the front door as far as he can tell. He shuts the curtains and lies down in his bed, holding a volume of manga in his hands so that he can get some reading in before he goes to sleep. But he just lies there, looking at the pictures, too frazzled to read. He sits like this until it's time for bed.

Too scared to fall asleep on his own, he decides to take an allergy pill to make himself drowsy. The drugged feeling is enough for him to close his eyes and vanish into dreams. He's sure everything will be fine when he wakes up the next day. He's sure the feral girl will be gone and he'll never have to see her ever again.

In the middle of the night, Yusuke wakes up to the sound of rusty barbed wire scraping across the wood of his desk. He opens his eyes and looks over to the shadowy figure in the room, standing by his closet. Her breaths become louder and more rapid. Her fingernails scratch against the side of her leg like a nervous tic.

Yusuke has no idea how the girl got into his bedroom. The doors are closed and locked. She couldn't have gotten in through the window without climbing to the second floor, without stepping across his bed and waking him up. It's like she just appeared out of nowhere.

Thinking it must be impossible that it's the girl with the barbed wire hair, Yusuke throws the cover over his head and pretends she's not really there. He thinks he has to be imagining it. The stress has gotten to him and she must be a hallucination. She can't really be the thing in the shadows that he thinks he sees.

But as Yusuke hides beneath his sheets, he continues to hear her breaths, he continues to hear the sound of her barbed wire hair jangling against her shoulders. Trying to scan his room through the fabrics of his sheet, he's able to see the shadowy figure come closer to him. He hears her breaths grow louder as she approaches. Her footsteps are wet and muddy against the hardwood floor.

Yusuke's heart races as she closes in. He wonders if he should jump out of bed and run away. He wonders if he should turn on the light and see if she's really there. But before he knows it, the shadowy figure is climbing into bed with him. He can feel the weight of her knee pushing down on the mattress on his right side and then another knee crossing over his stomach to his left. Before he knows what's happening, the girl lowers herself on his pelvis, pinning him to his bed.

Yusuke doesn't dare pull the cover from his head. He can feel her breathing pulse through his body. He can feel the barbed wire draped over his arms and chest. His whole body is trembling. He doesn't know what he can do. He wishes he would've run away when he had the chance.

The girl leans forward, pressing her body against Yusuke's chest. Even though there's a sheet separating them, the girl still moves toward him as though trying to reach his face. He can almost see her through the fabrics. The light shining through the window is enough that he can almost make out the shape of her head as she leans in closer.

She doesn't bother pulling the covers away from him. She doesn't need to. While watching her through the fabrics, Yusuke whimpers in shock as the feral girl's face passes through his sheet, phasing into it like it wasn't even there. Then she kisses Yusuke right on the lips. Just a quick peck and pulls back. The act wasn't at all what he expected. It wasn't vicious or malignant. It was actually kind of nice.

They stare at each other through the sheet for a while. Her eyes are glistening, almost glowing in the dark like a cat's. There's so much loneliness in her eyes. Yusuke realizes she doesn't mean him any harm. She's just desperate for human connection.

When she comes in a second time, Yusuke doesn't resist. He opens his mouth and lets her kiss him. Strands of her cold barbed wire hair scrape against his neck and shoulders. Her long fingernails dig into his forearms through the sheets. But the act isn't entirely unpleasant. He imagined her breath would be terrible, but her saliva is strangely nutty and sweet, like she's been eating chocolate-covered macaroons. Her skin is soft like it's rubbed in baby powder, not dirty or gross as he assumed.

Her lips feel oily and wrinkled, but he kisses her back as though she was a girlfriend he passionately loved. He doesn't know why he gives in to her advances, but he can't seem to control himself. Yusuke is also lonely and desperate for the affection of another human being. He's never kissed a girl before and is becoming intoxicated by the sensation. The girl raises a hand to his face and caresses his cheek through the sheets. She sucks his tongue into her mouth and pulls him tight to her chest.

Before Yusuke knows it, the girl pulls away. Her face slips through the sheets and disappears. She climbs off of him and returns from where she came. After it's over, Yusuke gets out of bed and goes toward the closest lamp. There's a part of him that wants her to come back, to hold him and kiss him some more. But when he switches on the light, the room is empty. She's nowhere to be seen. He wonders if he hallucinated the whole thing. It felt so real, there's no way it couldn't have happened.

He double-checks the room, looking in his closet and under the bed, but she's nowhere to be found. He lies back down, disappointed that she's gone, wishing he could've kissed her for a few minutes longer. But then he thinks about what he's wishing for. He remembers who exactly the girl was who entered his room in the middle of the night. He remembers how creepy she looked when she was tied to the chain link fence. That was not the kind of girl you'd want to make out with or have anything to do with. He feels ashamed that he enjoyed it.

But he still wonders why she came to his room if it wasn't a delusion. He wonders if she just wanted to give him a kiss to show her thanks for helping her earlier that day. Perhaps it really didn't mean anything to her. Perhaps she didn't really want to kiss him or have anything to do with him. He goes back to sleep thinking about her and the flavor of her chocolate macaroon kisses still lingering on his lips.

CHAPTER
THREE

The next day, Yusuke is confused about his feelings on what happened the night before. It was both traumatizing and exciting. He both dreaded it and enjoyed it. A monster came into his room last night and could have killed him, but he also was able to kiss a girl. He's conflicted about whether he should be happy or scared for his life.

He takes the alleyway behind the old fire station on the way to school but the feral girl is nowhere in sight. The anticipation of seeing her again has him trembling. A part of him thought she might have wanted to kiss him again, another part of him thought she might hang him from a tree with a barbed wire noose around his neck. But even if she would show him more affection he's not sure he would enjoy it. He might have enjoyed kissing her in his room in the dark, but if he saw her in person, in broad daylight, she might be too terrifying and disgusting to get close to. She might make him want to run away in fear. He's both disappointed and relieved that she's nowhere in sight as he passes the old fire station.

Once he gets out of the alleyway, he sees Narumi and calls out to her. She looks back with a disinterested expression on her face, as though she's worried that Yusuke thinks they have some kind of connection just because they hung out for a few minutes yesterday.

But the second he says, "I have something to tell you," she perks up with interest.

"It better not be to protest your undying love for me," she says. "That's the kind of boring thing most guys say to me whenever I show them even the smallest amount of attention."

Yusuke shakes his head. "No, it's about the girl with barbed wire hair."

Narumi's expression changes immediately. A smile grows on her face.

"Oh yeah?" she asks. "Did you see her in the alleyway just now?"

"No, I saw her last night," Yusuke says.

Narumi nods her head in the direction of the school so that he can talk while they walk. She moves forward down the sidewalk and Yusuke catches up to walk alongside her.

"After you left yesterday, I decided to go home and get some wire cutters so I could cut the girl free," Yusuke says.

Narumi bursts into laughter. "Are you serious? You really did that?"

Yusuke nods.

"And she didn't rip your throat out?" she asks.

"No, she seemed thankful. She followed me home

and wouldn't leave me alone."

Narumi's eyes light up with excitement. "Are you serious? She went home with you?"

Yusuke looks down, kind of embarrassed, not sure if he can tell her what happened next. "She even appeared in my room last night. I saw her in the dark, hovering over my bed. You were right. She really is a ghost. She didn't come through the door or window. She just materialized in my room out of nowhere."

His words make Narumi excited. She smiles brighter than anyone's ever seen her smile before.

"Oh shit, you're being haunted!" she cries. "You really fucked up by helping her out. Now she'll never leave you alone."

Yusuke lowers his head. When she said it out loud, he realizes how stupid he was for cutting her loose.

"Did anything else happen?" Narumi asks. "While she was in your room, did she just vanish the second you saw her, or did she try to attack you or something?"

Because Narumi is so excited, he realizes he can't let her down. He can't lie about what happened. But it's so embarrassing to admit that he doesn't know if he should reveal the truth.

Before he has a chance to come up with another story, he finds himself saying, "She came to my bed and started kissing me."

This causes Narumi to freak out in exhilaration.

"Are you fucking kidding me?" she exclaims. "She kissed you?"

Yusuke nods. He can't help but crack a smile after

he says that out loud. He can't believe he actually kissed a girl, even if she was a ghost.

"It was terrifying," Yusuke says. "I couldn't get away. I thought she was going to kill me."

"But you made out with the girl with barbed wire hair!" Narumi cries. "That's so fucking badass! Who else can say they did that? You're so lucky."

Yusuke is happy that she's excited for him, but he doesn't necessarily share her enthusiasm. He definitely doesn't feel lucky.

"But you said I'm being haunted," he says. "Isn't that a bad thing?"

"Oh yeah, there's no way you're getting rid of her now that you stole her first kiss. She'll probably haunt you for life."

Yusuke's eyes shudder in panic. "Are you serious?"

"Don't be scared. She probably won't kill you as long as you keep her happy."

"Don't mess with me."

"I'm not joking. She's a dangerous spirit. If you reject her now she'll tear out your throat without hesitation. Girls don't like having their emotions toyed with."

"But she's the one who came into my room and kissed me without my permission."

"And did you resist her? When she kissed you, did you kiss her back?"

Yusuke lowers his eyes. He definitely kissed her back.

Narumi pats him on the shoulder. "See. By doing that you reciprocated her feelings. Without words, you agreed to be her boyfriend. Trust me. I know what I'm talking about."

Yusuke slinks over, feeling depressed over the situation. He hoped he'd never see the girl again but if what Narumi is saying is true he's going to have a very hard time getting rid of her.

"What am I supposed to do now?" he asks.

Narumi smiles. "Give her your love. That's probably all she wants. Maybe she'll even pass over to the other side after you date her for a while. Maybe her desperate need to feel love from a quiet boy like you is what kept her here after she died."

Yusuke thinks about it for a moment and agrees that it's possible what she's saying is true. Maybe the girl with the barbed wire hair really does just need to feel the love of another human being in order to pass on.

"But how long am I going to have to deal with her before she moves on?" Yusuke asks.

Narumi thinks about it for a second. "Maybe once she feels your true love for her? You can't just kiss her or tell her you love her, you have to really believe it yourself."

"But how am I supposed to do that?"

Narumi shrugs. "I don't know. Might never happen. Either way, just be nice to her. She won't kill you as long as you're nice to her."

Yusuke has a hundred more questions to ask her, but the next thing he knows they've already arrived at the school. Before he has the chance to ask another question, Narumi's friends are calling her over and she runs off without even saying goodbye. Yusuke has no choice but to figure it all out for himself.

That night, the girl with the barbed wire hair returns to Yusuke's bedroom while he's sleeping. He's woken up by the sensation of her crawling into bed with him. He didn't even hear her anywhere in the room, as though she just materialized right above him and dropped down from the ceiling on top of his body. Yusuke gasps in shock when she appears, but then holds his tongue. As Narumi said, she might kill him if he rejects her. He has to pretend he likes her if he hopes to survive.

Yusuke doesn't have a chance to pull the covers over his head before she's on top of him. From the street lights coming in from the window, he can see her face more clearly than the night before. She just glares at him with deep sunken eyes. Her oily skin glistening in the moonlight. She doesn't smile or act happy to see him. She just looks at him as though completely emotionless and disinterested.

The girl is far more frightening in the light. Yesterday went by so quickly that he didn't get a chance to be too scared. This time it's incredibly upsetting for Yusuke. She looks like a demonic spirit from an old horror movie, the ghostly figures with pale white skin and wet black hair in their eyes. There are cuts all across her gray-skinned face, all caused by the jagged bits in her hair. Blood trickles down from her temples and neck. Her fingernails dig into his arms as she leans closer, holding him down with her weight.

She doesn't do anything for a while. She just lies on

him, her wet school uniform soaks through his pajamas. Her hot breaths blow against his neck through her nostrils. She glares at him with widened black eyes.

The girl doesn't seem like she wants to kiss him again. She seems like she just wants to be close to him, to warm herself on his body. But her eyes are so wide and alert, like she's just as alarmed as he is to be curled up on top of him. She's like a rattlesnake coiled on his chest, ready to strike at any second if he makes the wrong move.

Yusuke wonders if she's testing him, waiting to see how he reacts. If he responds negatively, with fear or anger toward her, maybe she'll runaway or decide to hurt him. If he responds positively, like he's happy to see her or excited to have her in his bed, maybe she'll let him live. But Yusuke doesn't like either of these options. He doesn't want to offend her or give her the wrong impression of him.

He decides to just stay as calm as possible and see if he can't communicate with her. Maybe that's all she wants—somebody to talk to.

"Hi there," he says, his voice slightly louder than a whisper. "My name's Yusuke."

She continues staring at him.

"What's your name?" he asks.

Silence for a moment, then a whispering sound comes from the girl's lips. Yusuke can't tell if she's trying to speak or just breathing hoarsely. He listens carefully but can't make out any words.

"I can't hear you," he says. "Are you trying to say something?"

The girl whispers louder, repeating herself. She speaks just loud enough for Yusuke to realize she's saying complete gibberish. None of her words are real words. He wonders if she's forgotten how to communicate. Maybe she doesn't even remember her own language.

Yusuke is becoming uncomfortable beneath her. The barbed wire is digging through his pajamas and poking into his skin. Her weight is getting heavier, making it difficult for him to breathe.

The odors she emits are strong enough to fill the room, perhaps even seep into the hallway. They aren't pungent or rotten, not as bad as somebody who hasn't bathed in weeks. She smells more like rainwater and river clay, like metal and car engine oil. But she also smells kind of like lime peels and mint leaves. It is not unpleasant, but it's overwhelming all the same.

"You're friendly, aren't you?" Yusuke asks. "You're not going to hurt me, right?"

The girl just continues to stare at him for a while longer. Then she lowers her face to his chest and closes her eyes. She rests her hand on his shoulder and just lies there, holding him close.

With the barbed wire centimeters from his face, Yusuke doesn't know what to do. She snuggles deeper into his pajamas, nestling her cheek into his pectoral muscles, then goes to sleep on top of him. Yusuke doesn't know what to do. She doesn't move. Her drool creates a wet spot on his sheets. Her breaths are slow and steady.

Yusuke can feel her heartbeat pulsing through him. He's not sure why she even has a heartbeat. He's not sure why she's so warm or why she is sleeping or why she breathes. She's supposed to be a ghost. Why would a wandering spirit do any of these things?

Not sure what else to do, Yusuke closes his eyes and tries to go to sleep. She doesn't seem like she'll leave on her own and he doesn't dare to push her out of bed and force her to go away. So he just tries to sleep. If he can fall unconscious he won't have to endure this anymore.

Yusuke wakes to the sensation of cold lips against his neck. His eyes shoot open. The feral girl is unbuttoning his pajama top, her long fingernails poking into his ribs. His body tenses up as he realizes she's naked beneath the covers with him. He can feel her school uniform bunched up at his feet. Even though he can't see her body under the blanket, he can feel her warm naked abdomen against his hands.

When the girl realizes Yusuke's awake, she lunges at his mouth and kisses him deeply. She pushes two long tongues through his lips and explores the inside of his mouth. At first, Yusuke doesn't understand why she has two tongues until he realizes how thin they are. Somehow her tongue has been split in half. They move independently of each other, curling over Yusuke's teeth and slithering across his taste buds. They are able to grip his tongue tightly and pull it into her mouth.

As she makes out with him, the girl pulls off Yusuke's

pajamas and tosses them aside. Once they are naked together, wrapped up in his blankets, Yusuke's able to feel her full warmth against him. He can feel her breasts against his chest, her legs wrapped around his waist. Her skin is so soft and silky like she's coated in baby powder and cocoa butter. Even though her body is covered in cuts and scars and mud, her flesh still feels impossibly smooth. It would be a heavenly experience for him if it wasn't for the barbed wire.

Now that he's naked, there's not much protecting Yusuke from the girl's jagged metal hair. It's so heavy against him, like a pile of bulky bike chains. Even though they were cut shorter when he freed her from the chain link fence, the barbed wire seems longer than ever, like it grows from her scalp faster than normal human hair. Most of the strands of metal are draped over the blanket behind the girl's back, but as she makes out with him, wrapping her arms around his shoulders and pulling him close, the blanket begins slipping down. Once the covers fall to her thighs, Yusuke is met with a barrage of wires. They hook into his skin, poking his shoulders and neck. The girl seems so used to the metal punctures that it doesn't bother her at all. She cares only about kissing Yusuke deeper, even if it hurts him.

Yusuke cringes at the pain but he has no choice but to tolerate it. He surrenders to the girl's desires. When he feels himself becoming erect, the girl reaches down and grabs hold of him. The sensation floods Yusuke with adrenalin. He can't believe this is happening. When she brings him inside of her, he can't help but squirm and squeal. He feels like his innocence is being ripped away from him by some kind of unholy abomination.

The girl starts crying as she makes love to him. He's not sure if it's because she's in pain or because she's overwhelmed by emotion. Her tears leak onto Yusuke's forehead as she pushes him inside of her. She whimpers and moans. Her teeth bite at the air every time she thrusts forward.

Yusuke can't feel much pleasure from the act. He doesn't feel much of anything but the barbed wire cutting into his skin. The whole experience is painful and awkward. There's a part of him that is exhilarated by being able to have sex with a girl, any girl. Another part wishes it would end immediately.

The squeaking of the bed fills the room. The feral girl is crying out, loud enough that his mother can surely hear her. He's terrified of what would happen if his mother walked in on them. Would she be upset at Yusuke for having sex at such a young age or would she think he was being attacked by a malevolent being and try to save him? Either way, he's sure his parents would disown him if they found out. Even if it wasn't his fault, he still attracted the ghost girl to him. He's responsible for her following him home from school. And they couldn't allow such a tainted son to stay in their household. It would only invite more acts of horror and depravity. They would think he was cursed and needed to be purged before he brought misfortune on the family name.

Once her volume gets too loud, Yusuke tries to quiet her down. He hushes her. He asks her to keep her voice down. But the girl only gets louder, practically howling at the top of her lungs. When Yusuke tries to get up, tries to separate from her, the girl holds him down. She seems to be reaching orgasm.

As her body begins to pulse and shiver, her hair comes alive. The strands of barbed wire grow longer from her scalp, moving on their own. They coil around Yusuke's arms and neck, they tie him up to the posts of his bed. The metal spikes pierce his flesh and cause him to cry out. The barbed wire doesn't stop even after he's tightly bound. It continues pouring out of her head, moving like vines if they were capable of growing at a lightning pace. The metal wires flow down the bed and across the carpet. They climb up the walls.

When the feral girl is finished, she drops down onto Yusuke and curls around him. She doesn't remove the barbed wire cutting into his limbs and throat. She leaves him bound to the bed as she holds him close, panting against him. Her heart races in line with his.

They stay that way for another hour and then the girl fades away. It's like she sinks down into the bed, into Yusuke's body. The barbed wire dissolves. He still feels the pain of being cut. He's still bleeding, still covered in wounds. And he's still coated in her scent and her bodily fluids. But she's definitely gone. He's finally alone again.

Yusuke doesn't get much sleep after that. In the morning, he gets out of bed and draws open his curtains to see the horrific condition of the bed sheets. It's like something died in his bed. The covers are torn and punctured. The sheets are wet with black oily fluids. A bronze liquid, like rust water, has saturated his mattress. He has no idea how he's going to explain this to his mother. It looks disgusting. It smells horrible.

Realizing he has to at least try to wash his sheets before he heads off for school, Yusuke pulls his bedding from the mattress and removes his pillow cases. Because his mother has already headed off to work by now, he doesn't have to worry about how to explain anything. As long as he gets the sheets clean.

As he brings the bundle of laundry downstairs, he notices something white sticking out of the blue sheets. Something that doesn't belong there. When Yusuke pulls it out, he finds himself holding a pair of women's underwear. They look old and gray, soiled with metallic oils. It's not the style of underwear that is available to buy anymore, not since several decades ago. Even though the girl vanished and took her school uniform and barbed wire with her, she left her panties behind for some reason. It's like she did it on purpose, as though it's a message that she plans to come back again soon to retrieve them.

After the sheets are in the laundry, Yusuke eats breakfast and gets ready for school. As he brushes his teeth and runs the hot water, he sees a shadowy figure through the curtain. Looking carefully, Yusuke swears he can make out the shape of the girl with the barbed wire hair. It's like she is standing naked in the shower, waiting for him to join her. But when he pulls open the curtain, no one is there. He showers as fast as he can and gets dressed. Then he puts the laundry in the dryer and rushes out the door.

At lunch, Yusuke sits at his desk eating the bento his mom made him the night before, which mostly contains rice balls and leftover soba noodle salad. He's still shaken from last night. He can't believe it actually happened.

Narumi plops down in the seat next to him and pulls her lunch out of her backpack. The other kids in the room look in shock at the prettiest girl in school choosing to sit next to Zombie-chan, but she doesn't pay any attention to them. They stare and whisper, but nobody calls her out on it.

"I've got so much stuff to talk to you about," she says, breaking apart her wooden chopsticks. "You're going to love it."

Then she smiles. When Yusuke looks over at her bento, he sees that she eats well every day. Perhaps she even has a personal chef that prepares meals for her family. Her bento is filled with high-quality sushi and tropical fruits, all cut into shapes like stars and kittens.

Yusuke feels awkward with all the guys in the back of the room giving him dirty looks. He's not sure if sitting with the prettiest girl in school will give him popularity points or make everyone hate him. He tries to just ignore all the eyes on him. After what happened last night, he feels like he can tolerate anything.

"Like what?" Yusuke asks her.

While holding a piece of tamago sushi in her teeth, she pulls out an old yearbook and drops it on her desk in front of him. Then she bites into the sushi and tosses the rest in her bento box.

"Look on page 117," she says, chewing with her mouth open.

Yusuke pushes his food aside and opens the book. He flips to the page, wondering what he's looking at. There are dozens of photos of students from long ago.

"Right there," Narumi says, pointing at a picture of a girl with long black hair covering most of her face.

"What?" Yusuke asks.

"That's her," she says. "Akiko Mori. That's the girl with the barbed wire hair."

Yusuke's eyes widen.

Narumi smirks like she's overly proud of herself. "It's definitely her. She went missing in 1983. I asked around everywhere. The stories all started with her."

"You really think so?" he asks.

Narumi picks up the book and holds it closer to Yusuke's face. "Look closely. It looks exactly like her."

Upon closer examination, Yusuke can see the resemblance, especially in the eyes. He was looking into those eyes for a long time last night. They are burned into his memory. He'd never forget them. The girl's eyes were just as wide and alarmed as they are in this picture, as though she had always been in a state of feeling constantly under attack. She looks so sad and scared. She probably wasn't a popular girl in school. Although she doesn't have barbed wire hair in this picture, and her uniform isn't ripped or dirty, it's definitely her.

"I think you're right," he says.

"I also learned more about the legend," Narumi continues. "I heard that the girl with the barbed wire hair only shows herself to people who attend this school. If you're too old or too young or attend a different junior high, you won't see her even if you go down the alley behind the old fire station. That's why I wasn't able to find her when I tried as a kid. It's also why cops and maintenance workers can take that path without trouble either. They say she was treated terribly by the other students when she went to school here. They say she wants to take out her revenge on anyone who attends our junior high, so that we can pay for the sins of her old classmates. She probably doesn't even realize that her bullies all graduated decades ago."

Yusuke can't take his eyes off the girl's photo. It's like her spirit is in the picture and she's looking out of the page at him, her soul piercing into his.

As he examines the yearbook, Yusuke doesn't realize the cuts on his wrists are showing. Narumi notices them immediately. Yusuke had been trying to hide them all day. He didn't want to have to explain the marks to anyone. But without thinking, he let his guard down long enough for her to catch on.

"What is that?" she asks.

Narumi grabs his arm and pulls up the sleeve of his uniform, revealing all of the fresh wounds up his arms.

She lets go before any of his blood gets on her hand.

"Did she visit you again last night?" she asks.

Yusuke hesitates for a second, but then nods. "Yeah. She was with me almost the whole night."

Narumi's eyes light up. "Seriously?" She laughs with excitement. "What happened? I've got to know."

Yusuke looks around, making sure nobody else is listening.

"She crawled into bed with me," he says.

"Oh yeah?" she says. "Did she kiss you more? Did she have her way with you?"

Yusuke nods his head and breaks eye contact.

"Bullshit," Narumi says, pushing him a little. "Don't make up anything like that."

"I have proof," he says.

"Oh yeah?"

He picks up his backpack and hands it to her. "Look inside."

Narumi does as he asks. She digs through his textbooks and papers, looking for what he's talking about. When she finds the underwear, she lifts them out of the bag and nearly chokes on her laughter.

"Are you fucking shitting me?" she cries. "Are these her panties?"

Yusuke nods.

"Holy shit! That's so crazy!" She stretches out the panties with excitement. "You actually slept with her, you total pervert!"

She smells them a little, just to verify that they've really been worn by a girl recently and weren't stolen from a store or laundromat, then recoils from the scent. It only takes her a minute to decide that they're the real deal.

"Why did you take them to school with you?" she asks. "That's so weird!"

"I didn't want my mom to find them," he says.

Narumi stands up on her chair and holds the panties over her head. "Check it out, everyone! These panties belong to the girl with the barbed wire hair! Zombie-chan had sex with her last night! Isn't that crazy!"

The other kids in the class stop talking to focus on what she's saying. Some of them giggle, but they don't seem to believe her or know what she's talking about. They just seem confused about why a girl would be holding up a pair of panties in the middle of class.

She looks down at Yusuke, "You lost your virginity to a fifty-year-old ghost!"

She sits back down in her seat and continues to fondle the underwear, examining its condition and design like she would a valuable antique. "You really impress me, Zombie-chan. Several guys at this school have already lost their virginities, but none of them can say they did it with a spirit, especially not the girl with the barbed wire hair. Guys like Hiroto are terrified of her and you go and steal her heart."

Yusuke snatches the underwear as she spins them on her finger and stuffs them in his backpack. "It's not something I asked for."

"Didn't you have a good time though?"

Yusuke holds up his bloody arms. "Do you think this was fun? My whole body is torn up from her barbed wire.

She tied me to my bed with her hair as she did it to me."

"Whoa…" Narumi snickers. "I had no idea she was so kinky. She must have been really into hentai before she died. Have you ever seen the old tentacle porn they used to make back then? It was pretty nuts."

Yusuke doesn't share her enthusiasm. He's riddled with guilt about what happened.

"But isn't she too young to want to do that kind of stuff? I didn't think girls our age were okay with having sex if they had any respect for themselves."

Narumi glares at Yusuke. She's obviously had sex a few times before, even though she's only fourteen. It's clear she doesn't have any problems with that. She doesn't like that Yusuke would assume that girls who slept with guys did so because they didn't have any self-respect. But even though she's offended, she doesn't call him out for misspeaking. It takes a lot more than that to rile her up.

"She's never going to grow up," Narumi explains. "She's already dead. She's probably been waiting decades to find a guy she could actually have a sexual encounter with." She pats him on the head. "Consider yourself lucky."

Yusuke pulls his head away, getting annoyed by her words.

"I can't wait to see where this goes next," Narumi says, popping another piece of sushi in her mouth. "This is the most interesting thing to happen all year." She chews and swallows, then eats a flower-shaped carrot chip. "I wonder if you'll fill her heart with so much love that she'll finally be able to rest in peace. Or maybe you'll fuck it up and we'll find you dead one day, hanging from a tree outside of the school."

Yusuke trembles at the thought of the dangerous situation he's found himself in. He can't believe it's a possibility that he might end up dead just by attracting the attention of a feral ghost, just by being nice to her and trying to help her out.

Narumi shrugs and says, "But if I had to place a bet on it, I'd guess she'll eventually kill you so that she can spend the rest of eternity by your side. That's what I would do if I was a lonely ghost who found a boy I liked."

When lunch is over, Yusuke is about to hand the yearbook back to Narumi when something grabs his attention. One of the names in the list of students is familiar. It's the same name as his mother's. He examines the photograph next to the name and is sure that it's her. His mother was a student at the same time as Akiko. She was a classmate of the girl with the barbed wire hair.

"You can keep it," Narumi says before Yusuke hands her the yearbook. "Every guy should have a picture of his darling sweetheart."

She giggles and then gets to her feet, taking the rest of her lunch back to her own desk.

CHAPTER
FOUR

Yusuke can't get the thought of his mother being a classmate of Akiko out of his head. He can't believe that she knew the girl with the barbed wire hair back when she was alive. She seemed to know exactly what Yusuke was talking about when he brought up the feral girl the other day, but he assumed she was only familiar with the urban legend. If she went to school with Akiko, she must know a lot more than the stories. She at least has to know what kind of person she was when she was alive.

When he gets home from school, Yusuke fingers through the yearbook, searching for more pictures of Akiko and his mom. The two of them are in several photos together. They were both in the poetry club at the same time. Yusuke knew his mother used to write poetry a lot when she was younger, before she had a career. She even published a book of poems when she was in college. But he had no idea she was in the club in junior high.

There are also photos of them performing together at the cultural festival. They appear to be on a stage, doing a reading together. In every photograph, there seems to be something off about Akiko. She's always hunched over a little, her eyes stretched wide open like she's permanently in a state of shock, her long black hair hanging over her face like she's trying to hide from the world. But in the pictures with Yusuke's mother, she appears to be a bit more lively and happy, even if by just a tiny bit. Yusuke wonders if they were good friends.

When Yusuke's mother comes home from work, he decides to confront her about her history with Akiko. He waits on the couch for her, nervously watching the clock and trying to prepare how he should approach the situation.

Yusuke's always been afraid of confrontation, especially when it comes to his parents. His father never likes to be bothered by anything. He cares only about efficiency and results and hates complications, especially when those complications are based in emotion. His mother is even worse to deal with than his father. Whenever he comes to her with a problem, she is always quick to get angry with him for having any problems at all, pointing out every flaw in his personality that led him to the dilemma in the first place. The criticism always crushes his confidence and puts him in a worse place than he was before asking for help.

"Why aren't you studying?" his mother says the second she walks through the doorway to find him lounging on

76

the couch like he has nothing better to do.

Yusuke sits up straight with a serious expression on his face. He doesn't apologize for skipping his school work. He knows that the only way to get through to his mother is to speak in a stern tone, present the information in the most formal way possible, or else she will brush him off and won't even listen to him.

"I have something to talk to you about," he says to his mother.

His mother comes inside and closes the door. She takes off her shoes and steps up into the living room.

"What is the problem?" she asks.

He raises up the class of 1983 yearbook and asks, "I have some questions about your time in junior high."

His mother's expression becomes severe. She charges to Yusuke and pulls the book from his hands.

She flips through the pages, asking, "Where did you get this? I thought I threw away my old yearbooks ages ago."

"It's not yours," Yusuke says. "A friend of mine gave it to me. I want you to tell me about Akiko Mori."

His mother's eyes widen when she hears that name. She grips the yearbook tightly in her fingers but doesn't speak.

"She was a friend of yours, wasn't she?" Yusuke asks. "You were in the same homeroom class and were in poetry club together. You must have known her before she died."

His mother shakes her head. "It was a long time ago. I don't want to talk about her."

"But she's the girl with the barbed wire hair, isn't

she?" Yusuke asks. "That's what I heard. She's the ghost that I keep seeing on the way to school every day."

His mom raises her voice. "I told you to stay away from that girl."

"I tried to, but—"

His mother interrupts him. She goes closer to him and looks him directly in the eyes as she speaks. "Listen to me, Yusuke. Don't take the shortcut to school anymore. She's dangerous. You don't want to attract her attention."

"I've already attracted her attention," he says.

His mother shakes her head. "It doesn't matter. Just ignore her. Stay away from the old fire station and you'll be safe."

"It's impossible for me to ignore her. She follows me home from school now. She appears in my room at night."

Yusuke wants his mother to know how serious his situation is, but he has to be careful about just how much information he reveals to her. He can't tell her exactly how far things have gone. He can't admit that he's had sex with the girl.

When he explains this to his mother, she shakes her head. "That's impossible. Her spirit is trapped in that old alleyway. She can't leave. You must be imagining it."

Yusuke rolls up his sleeves and shows her the wounds down his arms. "She did this to me upstairs, just last night."

His mother's eyes tremble, shocked when she sees the state of his body. She unbuttons his school uniform and examines his flesh closer, groaning with both disgust and empathy as she inspects the puncture marks covering her son's body, especially the cuts around his wrists where he was tied up with barbed wire. Yusuke feels awkward having his mother look him up and down without his shirt on at his age, but he allows her to get a good understanding of what is happening to him. He needs to know all that his mother knows if he hopes to get out of his current situation.

"What did you do?" she asks, handing him back his shirt. "How did you anger her so much?" Before he can respond, she continues, "I hope you didn't insult her. I taught you better than to offend the spirits."

Yusuke shakes his head, explaining he didn't do anything offensive to the spirit. "I just tried to help her. She was tied to a fence, tangled in barbed wire. She was there all day while I was at school. So I got wire cutters and cut her free. That's when she followed me home."

The mother gasps when Yusuke says this, she steps back and covers her mouth with her hand. He's never seen his mother so terrified.

"How could you do something so stupid?" she cries.

Yusuke shakes his head. "I didn't know she was a ghost at the time. I just thought she was some runaway who got caught in some barbed wire."

"By cutting her free, you released her from the confines of the alleyway. Her soul has become tethered to you."

"Tethered?" he asks.

"She is bound to you. She will follow you for the rest of your life."

Yusuke can't believe how serious his mother is about this. He can't believe she's this intense. She's always been strong, like a stone. She glares at him with such frustration that he doesn't know what to say.

He decides not to react emotionally. He calmly asks her, "How do I get untethered from her?"

His mother takes a long deep breath and exhales slowly, staring at her son with shivering eyes.

"I'm not sure if it's possible," she tells him, stepping slowly away from him. "I don't know if you'll ever be safe again."

Yusuke's mother gets a Shinto priestess to come to the house to perform some purification rituals. It's an old woman who looks like she might have been ninety years old, dressed in traditional robes. She walks through the house, examining the walls and floors and ceiling. Nothing seems to interest her so she goes upstairs, something pulling her in the direction of Yusuke's room.

"It's an onryo," the old woman says when she senses the remnants of a dark presence near Yusuke's bed. "A very restless one."

The priestess looks Yusuke up and down, then glares in his eyes and points a finger at him with shame, as though she can tell what he's been up to with the spirit, as though he's the one to blame for all of this. But she doesn't call him out for it. She doesn't tell his mother what she sees.

She explains, "This room, this boy, they must be cleansed."

The priestess spends the next two hours purifying the house with water. She chants to the spirits as she has Yusuke stand in the bathtub and douses him with water. She sprinkles blessed water all over his room, his bed, his pajamas and school uniform. She puts bowls of salt in front of doorways and windowsills. Then she places paper talismans on the front and back doors, on every window in the house, and gives one to Yusuke to wear around his neck.

"Never leave the house without this," she says, patting the strip of paper dangling against his chest. "It will protect you."

When the old woman is done with him, Yusuke's mother takes her into another room and has a conversation with her. They speak for quite some time, as though they have a serious matter to discuss that they don't want Yusuke privy to. He hopes they don't discuss the sexual nature of his relationship with the ghost. It wouldn't end well for him.

When the old woman leaves, Yusuke's mother bows deeply and thanks her for coming over. Then she returns to her son and looks at him with a blanket of worry across her face.

"You still haven't told me about Akiko," Yusuke says to her.

She looks at him for a moment, as though still hesitating to explain anything to him. But she reluctantly agrees.

"Pour me some sake. I'll tell you whatever you want to know."

Per his mother's request, he gets the largest bottle of sake in the house, the one with the strongest alcohol percentage and the cheapest price tag. The sake is supposed to be reserved for those times when his father has his lower-class friends over and wants to get good and drunk with them. It's not the kind of thing Yusuke's mother would ever drink when his father was at home.

Yusuke fills a wide-mouthed cup and his mother drinks two of them quickly before she begins speaking. She points at the glass one more time to be filled and then Yusuke places the bottle down and sits at the table across from her.

"Akiko was a weird girl," his mother begins. "Her parents died when she was young and was raised by her uncle who didn't want anything to do with her. I don't know anything about her home life, but there were stories about how he would lock her in the attic and force her to do all the cooking and cleaning even when she was very young. She also had to act and dress like a kyabakura girl whenever her uncle's coworkers were over, forced to light their cigarettes and flirt with them, let them do whatever they wanted to her. But those were probably just stories. There were a lot of them. People even said she was the daughter of a demon and a prostitute, or she was abducted by aliens and they scrambled her brains. I didn't believe any of that. She always just seemed like somebody who didn't know how to act around other people. She was painfully shy and unbearably lonely. All she ever wanted was to have friends but she didn't have a single one. Nobody liked her."

"What about you?" Yusuke asks. "Weren't you her friend?"

His mother sighs and takes another drink of sake. "I made the mistake of being nice to her when we were second-years. All I did was give her my pencil during a test after she broke hers, and once I gave her half my bento when the other girls dumped her lunch out on the floor. But that was enough for her to think I wanted to be her friend. She latched onto me after that like a parasite, following me like a pathetic puppy dog everywhere I went. She followed me through the halls, she followed me home from school. She always tried to come up with reasons to talk to me, even though I had no interest in having anything to do with her. Once she joined my poetry club, there was no escaping her. She was always there, always trying to be my friend. We were seen together so often that everyone would mistake us for friends. They thought we were as close as sisters. Teachers started putting us in groups together, sitting us at desks next to each other. She became my performance partner in poetry club. She was such a nightmare to me back then."

Based on what Yusuke had experienced with her, it sounds exactly like the kind of behavior he'd expect from the girl with the barbed wire hair while she was still alive. Even after her death, she just seems like a lonely girl desperate for human affection.

"She ruined my reputation in junior high. I was

one of the smarter students and only cared to be friends with students who took their education seriously. Akiko was not one of them. She didn't have good marks. It wasn't just that she was bad at school, she seemed to lack basic common sense. She was gullible, scatter-brained, unremarkable. I hated her even more than the students who bullied her. But she was obsessed with me. I became her favorite person in the whole world and she wanted to spend every minute with me. It was disgusting." Yusuke's mother clenches a fist as she conjures up the memories in her head. "By our third year, her obsession with me only got worse. It wasn't just that she wanted to be my friend. She wanted to be my lover. She wanted to be my girlfriend. I wasn't interested in women in that way. I don't think she really was either, but she seemed desperate to make us something stronger than just friends. She used to try to hold my hand and walk with me to school every day. She would kiss me whenever I wasn't looking. She would even sneak into my bedroom at night and crawl into bed with me. The same room you sleep in now. It was a living hell for me. There was something seriously wrong with that girl."

Yusuke pours his mother another cup of sake but doesn't interrupt her story. He's interested in every word. He can't believe she's gone through such a similar experience with Akiko as he has. It makes him feel like she's the only one who understands his situation, although his mother only had to deal with her while she was alive.

His mother continues, "I never kissed her back whenever she tried to kiss me. I knew if I ever reciprocated her advances it would all be over, she would be in love with me forever. So I made sure to reject her whenever I could. I pushed her away, told her it was gross and inappropriate to kiss me in the way she was trying to do. But she always misunderstood me. She thought I just didn't want her to kiss me on the cheek and wanted a kiss on the lips instead. She thought I didn't want to kiss on the way to school and wanted to find a private place where no one else was watching. It was infuriating to me. I just wanted her to go away."

It's awkward for Yusuke to think that the girl who was in love with her when she was young is the exact same girl that is in love with him now. They share the same creepy stalker. It makes Yusuke feel uncomfortable at the thought of it, as though he has an intimate connection to his mother that he really didn't want to have.

"When other students saw her kissing me outside of the library after poetry club, that's when the bullying started getting really bad. We were targeted as lesbians and all the worst kids in school used to tease us. The girls wanted to ridicule us. The boys wanted to hurt us. I no longer felt safe. I would take the alleyway behind the old fire station to avoid the other kids, but they soon caught on and would wait for us there. They would tease us and bully us at first, but then they got more aggressive. They would force us to kiss each other. The boys would hold us together and shove our mouths into one another and not let us go until we opened our mouths and kissed with our tongues. It was humiliating. But the worst part was that Akiko didn't mind the bullying. She seemed to enjoy it. She liked that I was forced to kiss her in that way. It made me sick."

Yusuke's mother doesn't wait for him to pour her another sake and drinks it straight from the bottle. She chugs for a good three minutes before half the bottle disappears and she slams it on the table. Then she gasps, trying to deal with the memories flooding back. It's like she's blocked out this part of her life for so long that she never fully got over it.

"What happened to Akiko?" Yusuke asks. "I mean, how did she die?"

"Nobody knows how she died. Or even *if* she died. She just disappeared. I was one of the last people to see her alive, though. Just myself and three of the boys from our school who used to bully us. She disappeared into the old fire station.

"The old fire station used to have these tall fences around it covered in barbed wire. They put it up to keep the kids out of the abandoned building. Before I went to school there, the students used to play in the firehouse after classes were over. There was a fire pole that kids would slide down, private rooms with beds that couples would make out in, areas where kids would smoke cigarettes and get into fights. It became such a problem that they put up barbed wire fences two stories high.

"The day Akiko disappeared, the bullies were especially violent. They said they were going to burn us at the stake unless we could prove that we weren't lesbians. They said we deserved nothing but death otherwise. What they wanted was for us to make out with them. That's how we would prove we liked men instead of women. They wanted us to desire them more than they thought we desired each other. It was easy for me. I wasn't attracted to Akiko and wanted the bullying to end. I told them that I hated Akiko and wasn't attracted to her. I told them that I was only attracted to men. I proved myself by kissing the leader of the three boys. I kissed him with more passion than I ever let Akiko kiss me, even under pressure. But this didn't sit well with Akiko. She was upset with me for not resisting them. She had no intention of giving in to their threats.

"They told her that they didn't want her to kiss them anyway. They said they'd rather burn her like the atrocity that she was. They said the whole world would be better off without her. And I was so horrible that I took the side of the bullies. I chanted with them as they called her names and said that she should be burned. Akiko was so crushed by my words. She didn't care about the boys who wanted to hurt her. She was more upset by the fact that I took their side.

"She tried to escape them as they threw rocks at her. She climbed the chain link fence, trying to get over it into the fire station where she thought she would be safe. But when she got to the top of the fence, she slipped and got tangled up in the barbed wire. Her hair got caught in it, twisting it up until you couldn't tell where her hair ended and the barbed wire began. She couldn't get free. We all watched her struggle and cry as she attempted to unravel the wires and get over the fence. When she reached the other side, she was only twisted up even more in the barbed wires. It wrapped around her arms and face. She was hanging from the fence, unable to break free. We could hear her skin being cut apart as she hung there, her weight pushing the points deeper into her.

"The four of us ran away. Akiko's screams had gotten so loud and high-pitched that they scared us. She sounded like she was in so much pain. But I didn't know what else to do but run. The next day, she didn't show up at school. I told the teachers what happened, leaving out the part about the bullies so that they wouldn't come after me. I said she was trying to get into the old fire station and got caught on the fence. But when the authorities arrived, Akiko was nowhere to be found. All the barbed wire from the fence had been taken down. There was also a hole in the ground leading to the fire station's flooded basement. The theory is that she fell down there, taking all the barbed wire with her, getting it wrapped around her so that she couldn't swim or free herself. Then she must have drowned. There was no proof to back up this theory. Her body was never found. They even drained the basement to look for her, but there was no sign of Akiko. Even though there wasn't a body, we all knew she was dead. We all knew she was never coming back. I never felt more relieved and guilt-ridden than I was in the days that followed.

"I graduated soon after that and went to the senior high school across town. But it wasn't long before the stories of the girl with barbed wire hair started surfacing. Students at the junior high swore they had seen her stalking the back alley behind the old fire station. They said she was living there, searching for somebody that she had lost. I wondered if it was really her. I wondered if she survived the incident and was so traumatized with what had happened that she couldn't return to school, couldn't return home, and just stayed in the same place where she was hurt until somebody would come and make it all better.

"I searched for her back there a couple of times, but never saw anything. I felt her presence, but she wasn't there, not alive anyway. Then students at the junior high started going missing. They either just vanished after taking the alleyway to school or they were found hanging from a fence or a tree, wrapped in barbed wire. That's when I knew that it was Akiko's ghost. She was unable to rest, searching for revenge on anyone who crossed her path. The stories continued after I left town and went to college. They persist to this day. I never thought that you'd get wrapped up in all of this. We never should have moved back to this town, back into this house."

Yusuke's mother drops her face into her hand, rubbing her eye socket into her palm. She has drunk far more than she should have, far more than Yusuke's ever seen her drink.

"It'll be okay, though," she tells him. "Our house is safe now. You will be safe. I promise. Once you graduate from junior high, Akiko won't be able to find you. She'll become somebody else's problem. You only have one more year left. I'm sure you'll be alright until then."

Yusuke doesn't have any more questions for his mother and she doesn't have anything else to say to him. She's so intoxicated that she can barely stand up straight when she gets to her feet. Yusuke helps her up to her room and puts her to sleep. Then he cleans up the living room and gets ready for bed. He's more than a little shaken by his mother's story. He feels sorry for both his mother and for Akiko. He can't believe that the kids at her school were so cruel, even crueler than the ones he's used to dealing with himself.

Before he gets into bed, Yusuke sees the ghost of Akiko lingering outside of his window. She's holding herself up with her barbed wire hair, strung up like telephone wires from the roof of the house. The paper talismans are working, though. She's not able to get inside.

Yusuke stares into her cold, lonely eyes as she holds out her hand, begging him to let her in so that she can be with him, so that she can hold him once again. For a second, he considers it. He can't handle the sad expression on her face and wants to make her feel better. But then he remembers the pain of having her wrap him in barbed wire, the embarrassment of being violated by a girl from his mother's generation. He can't let her in. He doesn't want anything to do with her.

As she presses the palm of her hand against the window, leaving an oily hand print on the glass, Yusuke closes the curtain and turns off the lights. He lies in bed and tries to go to sleep. He can hear her outside, whimpering, crying to be let in. She scratches on the glass like a stray cat. But he doesn't give in. He just lies there, unable to sleep, unwilling to let her inside.

But even though he rejects her, she refuses to go away.

CHAPTER
FIVE

The entire house is encased in barbed wire by the time Yusuke wakes up the next morning. It was so dark that he thought it was still nighttime when his alarm went off, not a single ray of light shining into the room. But once he drew the curtains, discovering a wall of tightly woven barbed wire, he knew it was Akiko trying to find a way into the house to get to him.

Her metal hair has stretched out, crawling across the roof, down the walls, digging into the pipes and rain gutters. The salt in the window has turned black. The talismans are wrinkled and fading, just barely holding the girl's spirit back.

"What is happening?" Yusuke asks his mother as she opens the front door.

But she doesn't respond to him. She seems very hung over and late for work and isn't able or willing to hear him out. She opens the front door, revealing a large black mass of barbed wire, pulsing and shifting, almost like a barricade to keep them inside. Yusuke's mother doesn't seem to see any of it. She steps right through as if it's not even there.

"Look out!" Yusuke cries, the second she vanishes into the metal blockade.

But she still can't seem to hear him. As she closes the front door, two strands of barbed wire dart toward the entrance to get in, to keep the door from closing. But they are repelled before they can reach the inside.

As Yusuke gets ready for school, he can hear the wires scraping across the tiles on the roof. He hears them in the drain pipes as he takes a shower. They scratch on all the windows at once like an army of cats who want to be let in.

When he leaves the house, the barbed wire spreads open, pushed back by the paper talisman around his neck. He has a sphere of protection around him the size of three arm spans all the way around his body. He rushes forward, dashing down the sidewalk, trying to get away before the wires can catch him. Once he's at a safe distance, he looks back to see the state of his home. It looks like a colossal nest of jagged metal. It pulses and twists like some strange machine at a factory, like it's somehow alive. He doesn't see Akiko, but he knows she's buried in there somewhere.

The mass of wire hair is all moving at once, trying to unravel itself from the house. Akiko knows that Yusuke's escaped and is desperate to go after him, but the hair moves too slowly. It must have taken her all night to grow all of that hair and stretch it around the building. Yusuke takes a deep sigh of relief when he realizes it will probably take her hours to get the hair to recede back into her head. He's able to walk safely to school without having to worry about her catching up to him any time soon.

At school, Yusuke runs into Narumi and she convinces him to ditch class with her and hang out on the roof of the art building. He tells her the whole story that he learned from his mother, about what Akiko was like when she was alive, about how she disappeared, about the priestess and the talismans, about his house encased in barbed wire.

Narumi is absolutely fascinated by all of it. She lights a cigarette and leans against the ledge of the roof, a big smile on her face as she takes a puff.

"That's so cool," she says the second he tells her about his house encased in barbed wire. "I would have loved to see that. Think it'll still be there if we head over there at lunch?"

Yusuke shakes his head. "It was unraveling the second I left home."

Narumi frowns. "Well, maybe she'll do it again tomorrow."

Yusuke looks down. "I hope not."

Narumi turns around and stares over the ledge of the building. "So I've been reading about how we can help her move on."

Yusuke's eyes light up. "You mean get rid of her?"

"Get *rid* of her? She's your first love. I assumed you'd have more empathy for her than that."

Yusuke bows and apologizes, though he's not doing it for Narumi's sake. He apologizes just in case Akiko is nearby, listening in.

"There's three ways we can help Akiko-chan rest in peace. We either have to get revenge on the people who killed her, find her remains and give her a proper burial or have her consummate her love with the man she desires." She laughs at that last one. "I say we go with the easiest one first and have her consummate her love with you. If it doesn't work then we'll try one of the others."

Yusuke's face goes white. "You can't possibly mean that."

"Why not? It'll be fun. Don't you want to make love with your darling one last time before we send her to the other side?"

Yusuke shakes his head. "I already did it with her. That can't be the thing that will let her rest in peace."

Narumi throws the rest of her cigarette over the roof. "Not necessarily. She had sex with you, but you didn't do anything but lie there and take it. That's no way to make love to a woman. You have to show her that you want her just as much as she wants you. You have to be the one to instigate the coupling."

Yusuke takes a step back. "That's insane. It's only going to make her more obsessed with me. Showing her any kind of attention is what made her cling to me in the first place."

Narumi shrugs. "Well, it seems like the easiest option

to me. I'd have no idea how to get revenge for her. Your mother might be able to direct us to the kids who bullied her, but they could already be dead or live in another country by now. Besides, I don't know what avenging her death means. Would we get them put in jail? Murder them? Lure them to the alleyway so that Akiko can take care of them herself? I don't want to do any of those things, do you?"

"What about finding her remains and giving her a proper burial?" Yusuke asks.

Narumi groans and turns away. She thinks about it for a minute. "Yeah, I guess we can do that. It's going to be a pain in the ass though." She turns back. "You said she disappeared in the old fire station, right?"

Yusuke nods. "That's what my mother said. She says she most likely drowned in the basement, even though no body was ever found."

"Well, we'll try there after school," she says. "I'll go home at lunch and get some supplies. Meet me outside the shortcut when class is out."

Yusuke agrees. He knows that it's a long shot, but he has to try. He doesn't think he can last the rest of the school year otherwise.

Everyone sees Yusuke and Narumi together when they go back to class and give a lame excuse to the teacher about Narumi having a menstruation emergency that Yusuke helped her with. She says she sent him to the corner store to get pads while she waited in the bathroom. The excuse is so awkward that the male instructor doesn't pry any further and tells them to take their seats, even though it's obviously suspect that a male student would help her rather than a female teacher or another girl.

The other kids in class are all positive that the two of them were doing something that they shouldn't have been doing, like making out in the band room or having sex in a stall in the girl's room. It wouldn't be the first time for Narumi, but it's such a surprise that she'd do something like that with the weird quiet kid. All the girls in the class are shocked and disgusted, all the boys are jealous and angry. When Yusuke takes his seat, every male in the room looks like they want to murder him for getting with the prettiest girl in school.

The rumors about Yusuke hooking up with Narumi spread like wildfire and eventually get to Hiroto and his friends. Because they are in different classes, Yusuke doesn't run into any of them during the day but some of his classmates warn him that his days are numbered. They say Hiroto is out to get him and that he's dead the next time they meet. Yusuke has enough to worry about with Akiko after him. He doesn't need the toughest bullies in school looking to kick his ass at the same time. Yusuke's not sure which one is worse.

After school, Yusuke meets Narumi at the entrance to the alleyway. He left class as soon as he possibly could to avoid Hiroto and his friends, rushing out the school doors and racing toward the place where Narumi was waiting for him.

"You ready?" she asks as he arrives.

Yusuke nods and walks past her, heading right into the alleyway as though it was the safest place in the world he could be with Hiroto after him. It's the only thing he knows of that will keep the big guy away.

"I brought a shovel," Narumi says, digging into her backpack to pull out a 12-inch camping shovel. She unfolds it and hands it to Yusuke. "Just in case we need to do some digging."

Yusuke takes it and holds it like a weapon.

"I couldn't find any flashlights, but we can just use our phones. Do you have your phone on you?"

Yusuke nods.

"Hopefully we have enough battery power for this. We're going to be there all day."

As they walk down the alleyway, Yusuke keeps watch for either Hiroto or Akiko. He watches the trees and shadowed corners of the alley, expecting something to jump out at them.

"What will we do if we actually find her body?" Yusuke asks. "How do we give her a proper burial?"

Narumi laughs. "We don't have to do anything. We'll just call the cops and have them deal with it."

"But won't we get in trouble for trespassing in the old fire station?"

"My dad is on the police force so it'll be fine. Besides, the curse of Akiko has been plaguing this town for ages. The cops will be happy to be done with it. You have no idea what it's like being a cop in a town where so many children go missing. It's painful having to tell so many parents they couldn't find their kids, that they shouldn't expect to ever find them again. At least to them, we'll be heroes."

Yusuke nods. He imagines it would be pretty rough. He always thought the cops in this town were lazy assholes who didn't want to do their jobs, but they're probably just emotionally exhausted by it all. Since her father is a cop, Narumi probably knows firsthand what kind of toll it takes on a member of the local law enforcement like her father.

"Let's hope we can find her," Yusuke says. "I can't wait for this to all be over."

Narumi giggles at the scared expression on his face. "Ahh, poor Zombie-chan. You must have had it so rough." She grabs him around the shoulder and pulls him close to her. "But this has been fun, too, hasn't it? It's been invigorating for me."

She lets him go and laughs again. "I kind of never want it to end."

When they get to the old fire station, Narumi takes wire cutters out of her backpack and cuts open the chain link fence high enough for them to get through. Yusuke folds the fence over far enough for Narumi to get through, then he follows after. Most of the windows and doors are boarded up, so it takes a while before they come across an entrance that's easy enough to get through. There is a large window that's not boarded, the wood rotted off long ago and lies scattered on the ground below. It's a window Yusuke has seen Akiko through a few times before, back when he thought she was a homeless girl instead of a ghost. They smash out the glass with a rock until it's safe to get through. Then Yusuke lifts Narumi to the ledge.

As he's pushing her through the window, the skirt of Narumi's uniform goes over Yusuke's head for a moment. Her bare thigh presses against his cheek, her underwear only inches from his eyes. But Narumi doesn't get upset over it. She doesn't yell at him or call him a pervert. It's almost like she did it on purpose, just to tease him and make him blush. When she straightens her legs, the skirt is pulled from Yusuke's face and the awkwardness recedes. Narumi jumps through to the other side and he follows after, pulling himself up, trying not to cut himself on the glass.

"Holy shit…" Narumi says as she turns on the flashlight of her phone. "This place is so creepy!"

She giggles with delight as she scans the dark room.

It's the garage of the fire house, where the old fire trucks used to be located. Now it's just an empty room covered in dirt and mold. Weeds have cracked apart the pavement, growing up the walls and flowering in the middle of the room despite the lack of sunlight. A cloud of dust fills the room like mist. Things move in the dark corners as though wild animals have made it their home. The place hasn't been used in decades. It's a surprise they never tore the whole building down.

"This is straight out of a horror movie," Narumi says.

Yusuke realizes that she's not just using her phone as a flashlight. She's also recording it on video. She's documenting their experience like they're shooting a ghost hunting movie.

"How many people do you think died in this room?" she asks. "Akiko probably dragged them in here and stashed their bodies in the spaces between the walls. If they tore the building down I bet they'd find a hundred skeletons."

"A hundred?" Yusuke asks.

"At least!" Narumi cries.

Despite the look of the place, Narumi seems to love being here. She looks so happy, smiling and exploring every inch with her camera light.

"So where do we start?" Yusuke asks.

"Look for a way to the basement," she says, moving her camera toward him. "I'll film you."

Yusuke feels awkward being recorded. He doesn't understand what Narumi is doing.

"Are we making a movie?" he asks.

Narumi nods. "We have to document this. We're freeing Akiko's soul from her eternal torment. This is a big deal. Everyone will want to see this."

Yusuke looks into the camera, not sure what to do.

"Okay…" he says, looking around for a way to the lower level.

Narumi says, "Tell us about how Akiko went missing. Tell us about how she fell from the barbed wire fence and drowned in the basement."

Yusuke looks at the camera, then looks away.

"I don't like being on camera," he says.

Narumi laughs. "Don't be shy. You're Akiko's lover. You're the one who's going to free her soul. Tell us all about the love affair you've been having with the girl with the barbed wire hair."

Yusuke doesn't like the direction this is going. He thought they were going to search for a dead body together. He didn't know he was going to be the one searching while Narumi filmed everything.

Narumi turns off the video feed and lowers her camera. "Come on, you're ruining my movie. Talk to the camera like the host of a documentary."

Yusuke shakes his head. "I don't like this. Let's just search for her body."

Narumi pouts but lets him slide. "Fine. Go ahead and do that. I'll document."

Yusuke takes out his phone and turns on the flashlight. He moves forward, exploring the room. Strips of light shine through the cracks in the garage doors. There's a passage leading to the right and a stairwell to the left. He decides to check the stairwell first, to see if there's a way leading down to the basement, but it ends in a pile of rubble and dirt. The place is so old that the stairs likely wouldn't hold their weight if they tried to go up them. Yusuke doesn't know if there's even a way down to the basement. He's not even sure if a basement exists at all.

Narumi gets bored with filming and turns off the camera. She goes to Yusuke, looking around the deserted building.

"It's kind of sexy, isn't it?" she asks.

Yusuke has no idea what she's talking about. He looks over at her as she goes toward the fireman's pole farther into the garage. When she gets to the pole, she grabs onto it and lifts herself off the ground. She spins around it like a stripper, her sweaty palms making a squeaky noise as she revolves and lands on her feet. Her skirt slides up as her butt nearly connects with the ground, catching herself only inches away from falling.

"I always thought firemen were hot. Don't you agree?"

Narumi laughs at the thought of Yusuke finding firemen attractive. When she smiles over at him, Yusuke just sighs in annoyance. This isn't a game to him. He wants to free Akiko's spirit so that she won't come after him anymore. He thought Narumi wanted to help, but all she cares about is messing around. He's beginning to wonder why she wanted them to do this at all.

"Check this out," she says to him, staring up at the ceiling.

Yusuke follows her to the fireman's pole. He looks up into the hole in the ceiling that leads to the second floor.

When he reaches her, he gapes up into the opening and sees nothing but darkness. There's likely a large room up there, but even when they shine their phone lights up into the dark there's nothing they can make out but a big black hole.

"Creepy, isn't it?" Narumi says.

As he holds up his phone to the hole in the ceiling, Narumi leans in close, pressing her body against his.

"This is such a turn-on, Zombie-chan," she says.

Yusuke turns to see her looking deep into his eyes. He has no idea why she's looking at him the way she is. Instead of responding to her words, he looks back up into the hole, wondering if there's anything up there that might be worth investigating.

"This really is the most exciting thing I've ever done," Narumi continues, pressing herself closer to Yusuke. "I've always loved ghost stories. They've always made me horny as hell."

"Huh?" Yusuke says, confused by what she's talking about.

He looks at her and sees a feral hunger in her eyes.

"I've always wanted to do it in a haunted house," she says, running her fingers through his hair. "There's just something about them that drives me crazy."

She pushes Yusuke against the fireman's pole and leans in close to his face, her warm breaths hitting his lips and nostrils.

"I think it's so hot that you slept with a ghost," she says. "I'm so jealous. I wish I could experience something like that."

She puts her hand against his face, touching his cheek. Then she looks him up and down, examining him closely.

"You're actually kind of cute, Zombie-chan. I can see why Akiko likes you so much."

Yusuke has no idea what she's doing. She's the most popular, most attractive girl in school. He doesn't know why she's acting like she's into him all of a sudden. They both know she's way out of his league.

"Maybe sleeping with you will be kind of like sleeping with a ghost," she says, getting close enough to breathe in his breaths. "You wouldn't mind cheating on Akiko just once, would you? I'm sure she won't mind."

The next thing he knows, Narumi is unbuttoning his uniform and kissing his chest. She pulls off his shirt and shoves him against the fireman's pole. Before Yusuke knows what's happening, Narumi pulls back his arms and handcuffs his wrists behind his back. She pulls off his pants and underwear, stripping him completely naked. Then she steps back, lifting her camera to film him, a wicked smile crossing her lips.

"You're so gullible, Zombie-chan," Narumi says, laughing her ass off. "I can't believe you fell for it."

Yusuke is standing there, completely naked, handcuffed to the fireman's pole as Narumi films him on her phone.

"You didn't think I was actually going to fuck you, did you?" she says.

She moves in closer and pulls the paper talisman off of Yusuke's neck. She puts it on herself, hoping it will protect her instead of him.

"I just want to make an interesting movie and you were ruining it," she says. "Now we've got to try something else."

"Stop it!" Yusuke cries.

He squirms in front of the camera, trying to turn his body so that his private parts aren't being filmed. He can't handle the humiliation of anyone in their school seeing footage of him naked like this. They'll all laugh at him. They'll all think he's such a pathetic loser for letting this happen.

"Let me go," he says.

Yusuke tries to escape, but he's completely trapped. The handcuffs on his wrists are police-issue. Narumi must have stolen them from her father. There's no way he can get out of them. He pulls his weight against the fireman's pole, but it doesn't budge. Even though it's so old and the building is crumbling around them, the pole isn't weak enough for him to break it free from the foundation.

"I want to see if we can free Akiko's spirit the other way," Narumi says. "The one where she consummates her love with the man she desires."

When Yusuke hears this, he finally realizes what she's trying to do. She's handcuffed him to the pole so that he'll be defenseless, so that Akiko can have her way with him.

"This is going to be so much fun," Narumi says, holding the camera in Yusuke's face. "I can't wait to see what's going to happen."

Yusuke has no choice but to beg his classmate. "Don't do this, Narumi-san. Please uncuff me. Don't leave me like this."

She giggles. "I'm not going to leave you. I'll be here the whole time. I want to film her coming for you."

Yusuke shakes his head. "Don't let her get me. Give me back the talisman. Please, let me go."

But Narumi won't listen to a word he says. She has a bigger smile on her face than Yusuke has ever seen. She's enjoying every second of this and has no intention of letting him go any time soon.

It isn't long before Akiko arrives. Yusuke hears her before he sees her. The sound of barbed wire scraping against pavement as the girl's long strands of hair crawl into the dark garage. They scrape their way across the floor, crawling up the walls, searching for the boy who has been evading their owner.

"Let me go," Yusuke pleads to Narumi. "She's coming."

But Narumi has no intention of freeing him from his bonds. She films the barbed wire as it crawls across the ground, reaching out for the naked boy on the fireman's pole.

The strands of hair switch directions when they come close to Narumi, curling away from her to avoid the sphere of protection around the talisman on her neck. She giggles with glee as she sees it all happen before her eyes.

"Don't worry, Zombie-chan," Narumi says. "She won't hurt you. She just wants to be with you."

Then she bursts into laughter as the barbed wire curls around Yusuke's ankles and crawls up his legs.

"Please, Narumi..." Yusuke cries.

But the girl recording him is too focused on the supernatural occurrence to care about his appeal for mercy.

When Akiko appears, she's floating in the air, being carried by her barbed wire hair. She comes out of the shadows and descends toward Yusuke. Her eyes are as wide and haunting as ever, locked on him like he's her prey, like she's upset with him for protecting himself from her throughout the night.

"Look at her!" Narumi cries, filming the ghost with her phone. "She's so terrifying!"

Then she giggles with delight.

Akiko floats toward Yusuke, holding out her arms as if to embrace him. Her school uniform dissolves from her body, revealing pale white breasts and black pubic hair.

When Narumi sees her naked form, she can't help but laugh. "Holy shit, look at her! Look at her boobs and erect nipples! I can't believe it!"

But Yusuke can't handle her words. Even though it is a funny game to Narumi, this is horrifying to him. He's not entirely unattracted to the ghost's naked body, but he can't help but be disturbed by all of this.

Akiko wraps herself around Yusuke once she reaches him, curling her arms and legs around his naked body. She presses her lips against his and kisses him deeply, her split tongue curling into his mouth. He can feel her breaths hitting his face through her nostrils. He can hear her whimper and wheeze with relief to finally be able to touch him.

"Holy shit…" Narumi says. "Is this really happening?"

Yusuke can no longer see the girl filming him, but he can hear her. As Akiko kisses him, curls her hand behind his neck, Yusuke hears Narumi laughing her ass off. He can feel her watching them like some kind of supernatural voyeur.

"This is so fucking hot!" Narumi cries. "I can't believe I'm actually watching this!"

Narumi moves to the side of them to get a better view of their faces as they make out. She comes in close, not afraid of being hurt since she has the talisman on her neck.

"Kiss her like you mean it, Zombie-chan," Narumi says. "Give her all of your love. Show her you care about her. That's the only way she'll ever move on."

Yusuke doesn't know what to do. He doesn't think that Narumi knows what she's talking about. He doesn't think kissing Akiko back will do anything but attach herself stronger to him.

He fights against the handcuffs, trying to free himself from his bonds. But there's nothing he can do. His inability to move makes it easier for the ghost to caress his body. Her hands rub his back and neck as she kisses him. Her legs curl tightly around his hips, straddling the fireman's pole to keep herself upright.

The girl's breasts are warm against Yusuke's chest.

Her stomach pressed against him almost feels good compared to the cold breeze coming from the broken window. He always assumed that a ghost would be ice cold to the touch, but she's as warm as any living human girl. He wonders if it's just his imagination. He wonders if maybe her warmth only exists because she loves him so much, because her heart is beating again whenever she's around him. Perhaps it would be different if he was somebody she hated, like one of the kids she killed for trespassing in her territory.

"You two look so cute together," Narumi says. "I can't wait to see you make love." She comes even closer. "Come on, Zombie-chan. You don't even have an erection yet. Let her make love to you."

Yusuke starts to think that he's now become involved in a low-budget porno film rather than a ghost documentary. He has no idea what Narumi plans to do with her footage. He wonders if anyone will even be able to see Akiko on film. It could just be a video of Yusuke naked and handcuffed to a pole, his lips moving as though something is kissing him. Perhaps students at the school will see her if that's the audience Narumi intends for the video.

As Akiko kisses him, Yusuke finds himself enjoying it. He stops resisting. He blocks out Narumi's voice and her embarrassing comments. He finds himself kissing Akiko back. Even though he can't move his arms, he imagines himself holding her as he wraps her lips into his. The moment he gives in and releases the fear in his heart, he can feel Akiko changing in mood. She releases his lips and leans back, staring at him with her deep sunken eyes. A small smile curls on her lips. Her eyelids relax, releasing her paranoid wide-open expression. She hugs him tighter and goes in for another kiss, one that's deeper and more loving than she's ever kissed him before.

Narumi vanishes in the background as the two make out against the fire pole. Yusuke feels Akiko's hair curl around his back, crawl across his arms and up his legs, wrapping him up like a blanket. It doesn't take very long. The barbed wire coils around them, creating a cocoon over their bodies. Yusuke's not sure if she's doing it to give them privacy from Narumi or if she's trying to keep him from escaping. The ghost girl's hair continues wrapping around them over and over until not even a speck of light can shine through. Yusuke can hear the metal wires encompass them until it's at least five feet thick.

It becomes hard for Yusuke to breathe. There's only a small space around his face, just enough for Akiko to kiss him and lick him from his neck to his eyebrows. The barbed wire pierces into his skin, cutting him from his toes to his ears, it weaves through his skin like she's trying to sew them together. But for some reason, it's not as painful as it has been in the past. The more love he puts into his kisses, the less the barbed wire hurts him. It becomes a motivation for him to forget that Akiko is a restless spirit and think of her instead as a girl that he's in love with. If he imagines hard enough, she can be the girlfriend of his dreams. She can be somebody he wants to be there with, somebody he can love forever.

It seems like days that Yusuke's been trapped here. The barbed wire's so thick that he can't hear anything on the other side. Narumi surely got bored and left long ago, leaving him alone in the abandoned building that nobody ever goes to. It's the most hidden, isolated part of town. He wonders if anyone will ever find him.

Even though it's been such a long time, Akiko seems to have no intention of letting him go. She will kiss him for hours at a time, sucking on his lips and tongue until they go numb in his mouth. When she gets bored, she nuzzles her face into the crook of his neck and goes to sleep. Then hours later she wakes up and kisses him some more.

Yusuke has urinated himself twice, but it doesn't seem to bother the girl with the barbed wire hair. He's so parched from not being able to drink anything, so hungry from going without dinner. He wonders how his mother is doing, wondering how worried she is of him. He wonders if Akiko plans to keep him there until he dies so that he'll be able to stay with her for all eternity.

After a few days, the police arrive and uncuff Yusuke from the fireman's pole. They are able to pull him right out of the cocoon of barbed wire, rip him out of the ghost girl's arms because to them she's not even there. She shrieks and screams to get him back, but the authorities can't hear her. The garage doors of the fire station have been torn down, filling the room with light. Yusuke blinks twice and watches as the policemen and paramedics try talking to him, trying to bring him back to the living. His throat is so parched that he can't get any words out. He's just thankful they found him before he died of dehydration. Every muscle in his body is sore from being held up by handcuffs and barbed wire for so long.

As they take him away on a stretcher, Yusuke can see Akiko trying to unravel her hair from the fireman's pole to catch up to him. But before he sees her again, Yusuke is put in an ambulance and rushed to the hospital.

He wakes up two days later, his whole body aching. Looking around the empty hospital room, Yusuke wonders what the hell happened to him. He has no idea how long it's been since he was last at home.

When the nurse comes into the room, she explains what happened to him. She says that a girl named Narumi called the cops after Yusuke hadn't been in school for five days. She says Narumi saw a couple of bullies handcuff Yusuke to a pole in the old fire house and leave him there, though she wouldn't say who they were, saying that she didn't recognize either of them. Then the nurse explains how terrified the cops were when they found him. They weren't just shocked he was still alive after so long without food and water, they were horrified by the state they found him in. He was raised two feet off the ground, floating in the air, not connected to anything in particular. It was as though something invisible was holding him up.

"But you're safe now," the nurse tells him.

She lifts his hospital gown to show him the tattoos on his chest.

"Your mother insisted this be done by the local priestess so this never happens again," says the nurse. "I'm sure your life will go back to normal soon."

Yusuke examines the ink embedded in his skin. There are three series of markings on his abdomen. They are each like the talisman that he wore on his neck but they are now permanently implanted into his body. He sighs in relief when he sees them. Even though they are now a permanent part of his body and can never be removed, he feels assured that Akiko will never be able to come near him ever again. They must have kept him safe while he was in his coma, otherwise, the ghost would have wrapped him up in barbed wire and pulled him out of the hospital room while he was unconscious.

But besides the tattoos, Yusuke also sees just how scarred up his body is. His arms and sides and the back of his legs are coated in wounds. He's so cut up and punctured by barbed wire that he looks like a burn victim. It's okay with him though. As long as he's alive that's all that matters.

When he's released from the hospital and goes home, both his mother and father are there to greet him. They don't look him in the eyes. They just say that they're happy he's alright and hope he can catch up on all the school he missed.

CHAPTER
SIX

It's raining heavily the next time Yusuke has to go to school. The second he walks out of the door, he can tell that something feels off. There are snails everywhere. They cover the road like pimples, sliding through the rainy streets. Snails are crawling up the walls of his house, crawling up trees and fences. Hundreds of them, like they are invaders from another world trying to conquer every inch of the town.

As Yusuke walks to school, he avoids stepping on all the little gastropods. He watches the ground, holding his book bag over his head to cover himself from the rain, careful to not crush any of them under his feet. He's never seen anything like this, wondering if it's even possible for there to be so many snails at once, wondering if they might just be a part of his imagination. But up ahead he sees some kids from school running through the streets, stomping on the snails with glee, playing with them like this is a normal thing that happens in this town from time to time.

Yusuke lets it go and rushes to class, but he doesn't

dare step on a single snail as he goes. He's sure it would be bad to hurt a single one of them. Just before he gets to the steps to the school house, he catches a glimpse of something behind him. It's just in the corner of his eyes, but he swears he sees strands of barbed wire growing out of the street like weeds.

Yusuke sees Narumi for the first time in days, but she just looks away the second they make eye contact. All the other students also look once they see him as he makes his way to his desk. It's like everyone in the school knows what happened to him, like everyone saw the video Narumi had recorded at the old fire station.

There's a lot of class work Yusuke has to catch up on, so he's not really able to follow what the teacher has to say on the current subject they're supposed to be learning, so he doesn't know what to do with himself. After class, he will get all the work he has to catch up on and then study his ass off at home. But for now, he just stares out the window and lets his mind wander. He hasn't really felt like himself since the incident. A lot of his memory of the past week and a half is missing and his body and mind just feel drained and yearning for sleep.

As Yusuke gazes out the window, he sees a figure in the school yard, peeking out from behind a tree. It looks like Akiko. She steps closer the second they make eye contact, holding out her hand as though begging him to come back to her. But the tattoos on Yusuke's chest are keeping her far away. Even if he wanted to be with her again, there's nothing he could do. She'll never be able to get close to him ever again.

But as the class continues, Akiko doesn't give up. She moves closer to the window, crossing the yard in his direction. It appears as though every step she takes is painful for her, like the power of the talismans in Yusuke's skin cause her to burn and writhe. But she endures the suffering. She advances no matter how much it hurts.

Yusuke isn't the only one seeing her come closer. Other kids in the class see the girl stepping toward the windows. They point and whisper. A look of panic spreads on their faces. When the teacher notices how distracted his students are becoming, he smacks a yardstick against his desk and yells at them.

"Pay attention," he demands.

But the teacher doesn't see what his students are seeing. He doesn't realize how much more threatening the feral girl is compared to him.

It doesn't take long before all of the students in class can see Akiko. They watch as her barbed wire hair spreads out, growing from her scalp and spreading across the grass of the school yard.

The other kids in class cry out and jump from their desks, backing away from the windows.

"What's wrong?" the teacher yells. "What are you looking at?"

He goes to the window and looks out, but doesn't see anything.

"There's nothing there," he says. "Why are you causing such a fuss?"

But the students ignore their teacher and back away, unable to remove their eyes from the ghostly figure approaching them. Narumi and Yusuke are the only ones who don't freak out about it. They both know why she's there. They both know she only wants Yusuke and there's no way she'll ever be able to reach him.

Before Akiko makes it to the windows, the teacher closes the blinds. He shuts them one at a time, blocking his class's view of the yard.

"Calm down," the teacher yells. "Get back in your seats."

Once the ghost is out of view, the students relax a little. But many of them are unwilling to go back to their desks.

The teacher has no choice but to threaten them. "Anyone not back in their seats in one minute will be subject to disciplinary measures."

Some of the students go to their desks immediately but others are more cautious, waiting as long as they can before inching their way back into their seats.

Once the teacher is satisfied and continues his lesson, all of the windows in the classroom shatter, and a wave of barbed wire oozes into the room.

The teenagers scream and fall over in their seats.

Even the teacher leaps back when he hears the windows explode. Though he can't see the barbed wire hair, he can see the glass flying, he can tell something dangerous is going on.

He tries to calm himself and speak as a protective authority figure, "Okay, class. Everyone exit the room in an organized, single-file line."

But as the metal hair empties into the room, curling around the desks and up the walls around them, the students scream and run out of the room, pushing each other over to escape.

"It's probably just a strong wind. There's nothing to worry about."

The second the teacher says this, one of the strands of barbed wire lashes out and tangles around a girl's neck. In an instant, her head is ripped off her shoulders and blood splashes across the desks, covering three of the screaming students.

The teacher falls to the ground in shock, some of the blood coating his glasses. Although he didn't see the barbed wire, he saw the girl die in front of him. He panics even more than the students.

"Run!" he cries. "Get out of here! Everyone out!"

Then he jumps over his desk and runs out of the room, not even waiting to make sure all of his students have made it to safety before he makes his escape.

It's not just in one classroom. All the windows in the school seem to have been broken open.

Yusuke steps out into the hallway, watching all the other kids running in a panic. They head for the exit, trying to escape before anything happens to them. But the barbed wire hair is already coiling around the doors, locking them inside.

"Your girlfriend seems kind of pissed," Narumi says as she steps up next to Yusuke. She looks at him with almost a smirk on her face, but even stone-cold Narumi can't help but show anxiety over the situation.

Yusuke turns to her. "You're the one who did this. I told you that she'd get worse if I reciprocated her feelings for me."

Narumi just laughs off his words. "I'm not the one who made her fall in love with you, Zombie-chan. You did that all on your own."

Then she lights up a cigarette, using the panic to get away with smoking in the hallways.

Yusuke scowls at Narumi. He's still pissed about what she did to him the other week.

"You left me hanging in the fire station for days," Yusuke says. "I could have died."

Narumi blows smoke at the students running through the hallway.

"I got you rescued though, didn't I?" she says. "If I left you there none of this would have happened. Akiko would have been satisfied. She would have been able to love you forever."

As the exit at the end of the hallway breaks open, a wave of barbed wire gushes inside. Three students disappear in the mass of rusted metal. The others run screaming in the opposite direction. As he sees some of them being ripped apart, blood splattering across the walls, he realizes that Narumi might be right. He realizes that he could have prevented all of this.

"Let's go," Narumi says, tossing her cigarette on the ground.

Barbed wire is crawling out from under the classroom doors, gushing down the hallways. There doesn't seem like there's any place they can escape to.

"Go where?" Yusuke says.

Narumi leads the way. As she walks, she says, "The auditorium is in the center of the school. There's no windows, fewer entrances. It's probably the safest place."

As they walk, it seems like many of the other students have the same idea. They run down the hall toward the auditorium, trying to escape the barbed wire crawling deeper into the building.

As they get to the auditorium, they're already too late. There is a mass of barbed wire descending from the ceiling like a spider's thread. It has latched onto five different students, crawling around their necks and pulling them up toward their deaths. The other students run in a panic, terrified of being caught by the deadly wires. When Yusuke sees all the dead bodies hanging from the ceiling, he realizes he's the only person who can stop this.

"I need to go to her," Yusuke says. "I'm the one she wants."

Narumi looks at him. "You really think that will be enough? She's been trying to take her revenge on this school for decades. This might not even be about you anymore."

"But so many people are dead because of me," Yusuke says.

Narumi pulls him close to her so he can hear her over all the screams. "You're not the one doing the killing. Don't take the blame for this. It'll destroy you if you do."

Yusuke is surprised by how calm Narumi is. He has no idea why she's trying to console him with all the death and destruction happening around them. But when he catches a glimpse at the paper talisman peeking out of the collar of her school uniform, he realizes why she's so relaxed. She knows she's safe. She knows nothing will happen to her. The two of them are the only ones who have nothing to worry about.

On the other side of the school, there's an exit where the hair hasn't reached. Hundreds of students have been able to escape that way. The flood of screaming kids going toward the exit knocks Yusuke to the ground and pushes

Narumi against a wall. Most of them are able to get out before the hair reaches the final outlet. But before Yusuke and Narumi can get out, the barbed wire curls into the doorway, weaving itself into a barricade.

There are still dozens of students trapped inside. All of the teachers have left the building, trying to escort everyone to safety. Because they couldn't see the hair, they didn't know exactly what the danger was. They led more than a few children to their deaths by telling them to go in a direction that had already been overtaken by barbed wire. But the teachers don't come back into the building, even though they are perfectly capable of doing so, even though they know more students are still inside. They've heard of the stories of the girl with the barbed wire hair. They don't quite believe what their students tell them they've seen, but they know not to mess with such a vengeful spirit. They won't go back into the building again without the place being cleansed by a priest.

"Hey you," Narumi yells to a group of students running from the barbed wire. "Come to us. We'll keep you safe."

Yusuke is surprised that Narumi would play the hero. She always seemed to be the kind of person who would revel in all the death surrounding them.

"How? What can you do?" one of the girls asks her.

"Trust me," Narumi says to her.

Some of the kids believe her and stay by her side, while others keep running. They take another hallway but are immediately overrun by a wave of barbed wire. Those that stick by realize the metal strands won't come anywhere near Narumi or Yusuke. They don't know about the talismans tattooed on Yusuke's chest or the one made of paper around Narumi's neck. They just know that they're safe if they keep close.

Yusuke and Narumi take a group of students to the band room. It's close to the center of the school. It doesn't have any windows and only one door. It's the safest place they're able to get to and secure from the girl with the barbed wire hair.

When they enter the room, there are a handful of students already hiding in here. One of them is Hiroto. His friends Itachi and Touma are with him. Despite how big and scary the three guys are, they all look tiny and pathetic when Yusuke and Narumi enter the room. They seem to be scared to death, even worse than the other kids around them.

Narumi closes the door to the band room and locks it. There's no one else out there. Everyone else in the school has surely drowned in the flood of twisted metal. Once the door is secure, they hear the barbed wire pile up outside, forming a barricade. It tries to get under the door but can't get too close, not with the talismans holding it back.

When Hiroto sees Yusuke, he can't help but feign toughness. He gets to his feet, stretches out his arms, and goes to the scrawny shy kid.

"You did this, didn't you?" Hiroto asks Yusuke. "You

pissed off the girl with the barbed wire hair. She's killing everyone to get to you."

Yusuke looks at the fear in his eyes, the anguish. He can't help but feel sorry for the large scared kid. He can't help but feel guilty about all of this.

"I'm sorry," Yusuke says. He bows deeply and holds it for almost a minute. "This is all my fault."

But his sincere apology only makes Hiroto angrier. He grabs Yusuke by the collar and pulls him upward.

"What the hell did you do?" Hiroto says. Spit splashes in Yusuke's face, but he just takes it. Even if he's punched in the face and kicked in the stomach a few times, he doesn't think it would be undeserved.

"He made love to the girl with the barbed wire hair," Narumi tells him.

When Hiroto hears this, he loosens his grip a little.

"He what?" Hiroto asks.

It's obvious the big guy never heard the rumor.

Narumi explains. "The ghost is in love with him. She's attacking the school so that she can get closer to him, because she desperately wants to be with the only person who ever showed her any kindness."

Everyone can see the confusion spreading across Hiroto's face. He has no idea how Narumi's words could possibly be true. But he doesn't question her. He lets Yusuke go and takes a step back.

Itachi speaks up. "Well, if all she wants is Zombie-chan I say we give him to her."

"Yeah, fuck that guy," Touma says. "He's responsible for all of this."

Hiroto looks back at his friends and then nods. All the other kids in the room agree. They all think Yusuke has to take the fall in order to save them.

"Okay, we'll give you over to her," he says to Yusuke. "If that's all she wants then it's an easy choice. You in exchange for all of us."

Hiroto grabs Yusuke again and pushes him toward the door.

"It won't work," Yusuke says. He unbuttons his shirt and shows him the three talismans tattooed on his chest. "She can't get to me because of these. It's probably why she's so desperate."

Hiroto examines the kanji inked into his skin and decides to believe him. Yusuke is surprised it was enough to call him off. He's surprised Hiroto would be so reasonable.

But then the bully says, "I guess we need to cut them out off you then," and panic fills Yusuke's face.

Hiroto looks over at his friends and they lunge forward. They grab Yusuke and hold him to the ground. Hiroto sits down on his stomach and pulls a box cutter out of his pocket.

"This is going to hurt," Hiroto says as he brings the blade of the box cutter to Yusuke's chest.

But before he can touch a single kanji, Narumi grabs him by the wrist.

"Are you a fucking idiot?" she says to him.

Hiroto is thrown off by the most beautiful girl in the school coming so close to him that he doesn't resist when she pulls the blade from his fingers.

"The kami in his tattoos is the only thing keeping

you all alive," Narumi says. "If you destroy the ofuda the barbed wire is going to break in and tear you apart."

Hiroto looks up at her. "But she only wants him, doesn't she?"

Narumi nods. "Yeah, and you'll be in her way. All of the barbed wire will flood into this room and kill everyone. She also won't be too happy with you hurting her lover."

When she says this, it's enough for Hiroto to pull back. He stands up and pushes his friends away from Yusuke. They let him get to his feet.

"Fine," Hiroto says to Narumi. "We'll do it your way."

The sound of crumbling and crashing echoes through the hallway as the school falls apart all around them. The entire building is encased in barbed wire and it is being tightened every moment they wait. The structure isn't able to handle it. The roof, the walls, it's all coming down. The students in the band room won't last in there forever, even with the ofuda tattooed to Yusuke's chest.

"We need to go," Yusuke says.

"How?" Hiroto asks. "We're surrounded."

Yusuke nods, but says. "It's a risk but I think I can get us out of here."

The others pay close attention to what he has to say.

"We have two options," Yusuke says. "Either I leave the room and exit the building, hoping that Akiko follows me and leaves the school before it crumbles around us.

Or we all leave together. If you all stick close to me, it's possible that she won't be able to touch any of you. We can get out of the building at least. Once we're free, all of you can run away and leave me to deal with her."

The group thinks about it for a few minutes, but it doesn't take them long to decide to go with Yusuke. Itachi and a few others don't want to go, but even they agree once the crashing sounds escalate around them. It doesn't seem like the ceiling is going to hold for much longer.

"You lead the way," Hiroto says, pointing Yusuke in the direction of the exit.

When Yusuke opens the door and steps into the hallway, a mass of barbed wire shuffles away from them. It takes a minute, but eventually, the passage is clear. Yusuke steps out in the hall and the other students follow behind him. He leads them toward the closest exit, barbed wire spreading out to give way for them.

Despite being the biggest and toughest of the group, Hiroto is the one who clings the closest to Yusuke. He nearly is wrapped around his hips as he follows him. The way the barbed wire parts for Yusuke is proof that he's protected from the ghost girl's curse. There's nothing safer than being by his side.

Akiko appears before they reach the exit. She comes up behind them, a cloud of barbed wire twisting like machinery at her back. She's naked as she was back in the fire station, her pale skin a haunting sight for the students who have never seen her before.

Everyone gets on the other side of Yusuke, protecting themselves from the girl with the barbed wire hair. A few of them separate and run for the exit. Two of them make it, but the third is snatched up by a lock of hair and pulled into the auditorium. It's unclear whether she is killed or not, but her screams fill the hallway for a moment before they are cut short, as though barbed wire crawls down her throat and suffocates the breath from her.

"There she is," Narumi says, her eyes locked on Akiko, a smile curling up the side of her mouth. "She tore apart the whole school looking for you and has finally come face to face."

Yusuke stares at Akiko, angry with her for what she's done. He tries to tell her without words how horrible she is for doing everything she's done. But Akiko just stares at him with her usual wide-eyed expression. She cocks her head at him and steps forward.

The people behind Yusuke inch backward, not wanting to get too close to the feral girl as she approaches. But Yusuke doesn't move. He stands in his place, waiting to see how close she can make it before the ofuda pushes her away.

"That's her," Hiroto says, pointing over Yusuke's shoulder. "That's really her. She's the bitch who killed my brother."

Narumi hushes him. "Don't offend her. She's very sensitive."

Hiroto becomes nervous. "She can't reach us, can she? We're safe by Zombie-chan, aren't we?"

But the talismans in Yusuke's chest don't hold her back. She pushes through the pain, moving forward as though she's swimming against a current.

"She won't rest until Yusuke is hers," Narumi says.

Akiko's hair flares out behind her, the barbed wire swirling and twisting, moving like flames against her back. The walls around her are torn to shreds as she walks, scraping against the wood in such a way that all of the students' ears tense up.

"Go to her," Narumi tells Yusuke. "It's the only way her soul will be at peace. It's the only way to calm her restless spirit."

Yusuke doesn't know why he's listening, but he decides to do as Narumi suggests. He steps forward, going toward the pale-skinned girl. The students behind him don't follow. They aren't sure if it's safe to let Yusuke get too far ahead, but they don't want to go any closer to the girl with the barbed wire hair.

"You really do like her, don't you?" Narumi asks Yusuke. "You're just as lonely as she is. You need somebody like her to take away your solitude. That's why she chose you. The two of you both belong with each other."

Although Yusuke doesn't agree with the words Narumi is saying, he finds himself opening his arms, reaching out for Akiko. The ghost girl goes to him and embraces him, fighting the pain it causes her as the talismans hold her back.

Yusuke kisses her the moment they reach, wrapping

his arms around her, his skin tearing against the shifting barbed wire. The two of them tolerate the pain of being with each other and fully embrace, filling the deep dark holes buried inside of them. At first, Yusuke is doing it just to save his classmates, trying to sacrifice himself so nobody else has to die. But then he realizes that there's comfort in Akiko's arms. Even though she's not human, even though she's been dead for decades, he lets in the girl's love. And for the first time since he met her, he gives his love back. He kisses her as though he means it, as though he really does want to be with her, spend his life or even his afterlife cradled in her arms.

The rusted barbed wire becomes thin and black. It falls to Akiko's sides, becoming human hair once again. As he holds her, Yusuke can feel the tears rolling from her eyes and down his cheeks. She releases him and looks him in the eyes. She no longer looks like a ghostly demon anymore. She looks like a normal girl, just a sad lost girl who's finally found what she's been seeking for so long.

The other students stand there, staring at them. They don't utter a word, just watching from a safe distance, hoping that it's all over.

Akiko and Yusuke turn around and move forward, walking hand in hand through the hallway. They pass through the students who spread apart to make way for them, watching the shy kid and the ghostly naked girl go through the exit and leave the building. All the teachers and policemen out front just stare at Yusuke holding his hand out in midair, unable to see the ghost girl he walks with.

The two of them walk all the way home together, not saying a word. Every once in a while they look over at each other and their eyes meet and Akiko lets out the biggest, brightest smile Yusuke has ever seen. They go to Yusuke's house and climb the stairs. The talismans protecting the building crumble and fall away. The tattoos on Yusuke's chest fade from his skin.

The two of them sit on Yusuke's bed and just stare into each other's eyes for hours. They lie down together, holding each other, happy just being with one another. Neither of them has ever felt so much love and acceptance as they do in this moment.

When Yusuke wakes up that evening, Akiko is gone, faded from existence. His parents come home, worried about what happened to him but he says he's perfectly fine. He tells them they don't have to worry about him anymore.

Narumi comes to visit him the next morning and they talk on the road out front of Yusuke's house. She asks about what happened after he left the school and he tells her about how Akiko is no longer with him. She faded away in his arms.

"I think she moved on," he says. "You were right. She just needed to consummate her love with someone. It didn't need to be sex. She just needed to feel loved by someone."

Narumi nods her head. "Yeah, maybe. Hopefully."

Yusuke is puzzled by her response. "You think she'll be back?"

Narumi shrugs. "As of today, the school has been closed down for repairs. We're no longer students there." She looks Yusuke in the eyes. "They're transferring us to the school across town. That means the curse no longer applies to us. We can never see Akiko ever again."

"You mean she might still be out there?" Yusuke asks. "Trapped between life and death. All alone?"

"Maybe." Narumi shrugs. "I don't know. But either way, she's gone. She might have moved on. She might just be invisible to us. We'll never know."

Yusuke sits down on the steps to his house and puts his hands on his knees.

"That can't be true," he says. "I saw her fade away. She has to have moved on."

Narumi nods. "Then that's what happened. Forget about what I said. I think it's better to think that her spirit is finally free, that she'll never hurt anyone ever again."

She puts her hand on Yusuke's head like he's a little kid.

"You did good, Zombie-chan. You helped her. No matter what, you should feel proud that you made that girl happy."

Narumi walks to the edge of the sidewalk and turns back. She says, "Sorry for forcing you through all that. Maybe we'll see each other in the new school. I'm sure you'll need a friend. I doubt any of the other kids will go near you ever again."

Yusuke nods and watches her as she walks off. She

waves without looking back at him.

Narumi won't see him in the new school, however. For the rest of the year, Yusuke stays home and takes classes online. His parents don't let him out of the house again until he's ready to go to senior high school. They are ashamed by the idea that their son was responsible for so many deaths, even if he didn't kill them himself. They blame him for everything. They also blame themselves. Once he graduates and leaves the house, they tell him that they'll likely never speak to him again.

PART TWO

CHAPTER
SEVEN

Yusuke gets into a good university and then gets a good job with a respectable company in the city. He moves into a small apartment and focuses on work and not much else. He works long hours. He only socializes with his boss and peers in the company but he doesn't like them very much. He's never been in a serious relationship after Akiko. He doesn't have time to go on dates.

The first time Yusuke realizes he's still being haunted is when he returns to his hometown for his father's funeral. He wasn't invited. His mother told him never to show his face in that town again, not with so many families blaming him for the loss of their loved ones. But he shows up unannounced and watches the ceremony from a distance, dressed in a way that he won't be recognized. He sees his mother briefly, but she doesn't notice him. She looks like she's grown old and hard in the past decade. She looks like she doesn't even know how to grieve anymore, at least not on the outside.

After ten minutes, Yusuke goes for a cigarette and walks around the block, looking at the surrounding buildings, memories he's forgotten flooding back to him. The town hasn't changed much since he left. It's a place that's always been trapped in the past, holding tight to its superstitions and traditions while the rest of the country grows and evolves around it. As he puts out his cigarette in an ashtray by the bus stop, he hears a commotion behind him. A group of school girls are crowded close to each other, gossiping with concerned voices, pointing in his direction.

"It's him," one of them cries. "It's Yusuke."

Yusuke looks over at them. There's no way they could possibly recognize him. They shouldn't even know what he looks like. They were probably toddlers when he moved away. He figures they must be talking about somebody else, even though there's no one else on the street.

"There she is…" another says. "Do you see her, hiding behind him?"

Yusuke listens carefully, trying to understand what they're saying to each other.

They continue:

"Her hair. Look at her barbed wire hair!"

A girl lets out a nervous giggle. "It's so creepy!"

"It's really them. They're really real."

"I can't believe the stories are true."

When Yusuke looks over at them, they quiet down. He steps across the street toward them and they back away, but they don't run.

"What are you talking about?" he asks. "Did you say something about a girl?"

The schoolgirls flinch and let out quick cries as

though something is lunging at them. They tremble in their shoes, holding each other tightly, but they don't respond to Yusuke's question.

One of them gets the courage to break free from the others. She steps forward and says, "She wants us to tell you she still loves you and she'll never leave your side."

Yusuke freezes for a moment. He opens his mouth to speak but his voice is a stutter.

When he finally is able to ask, "What do you mean by that?" the girls are already running away.

"Hey, wait!" he calls out, but they're already turning a corner and moving out of sight.

He doesn't follow after them.

Yusuke steps into a nearby coffee shop and orders an espresso. He nods at the pretty barista.

"The craziest thing just happened to me," he tells her. "These junior high girls just said something to me that freaked me out."

The barista laughs and nods her head.

"Did they see Akiko following you at the hip?" she asks.

When he hears this, his eyes go wide. He looks up at her, wondering if she's also a junior high student, wondering how she could know that unless she can see the ghost herself. But she's too old to be in junior high. She looks closer to Yusuke's age than theirs.

"It's been a long time, Yusuke," she says. "Don't you recognize me?"

Yusuke looks carefully. It's been so long that he had no idea it was the girl he went to school with back then. She's so much different than the girl he remembered.

"Narumi?" he asks. "Is that you?"

She laughs. He might not recognize her face but that laugh he remembers well. It is definitely her.

"What are you doing here?" he asks.

"I work here," she says. "I'm the manager, actually. Been here since graduation."

"Are you serious?"

When the espresso's ready, Narumi goes on break and they sit for a chat. She explains how she never went to college or left town. She dated Hiroto for a couple of years after school but that ended badly. And any other relationship she ever had after that didn't last long. Too many people knew of her involvement in the tragedy that took place in junior high. Everyone in town sees her as bad luck.

Yusuke feels awful hearing about all of this. He always looked up to Narumi. He always thought she would've been living a far more exciting and fulfilling life than himself. When he apologizes, she just shrugs it off like she's grown used to it, like she really doesn't care about anything anymore.

When Yusuke asks again about the school girls outside, Narumi says, "You've become kind of a legend since junior high. Everyone knows your story. The school kids sometimes come in here to talk to me about it. They want me to tell them the famous ghost story of Akiko and Yusuke."

She smiles in delight at the thought of it, like the events she lived through were among the biggest highlights of her life.

"But I've been gone for years," Yusuke says. "How are they able to see her?"

"Didn't you hear the stories while you were in senior high?"

Yusuke shakes his head.

Narumi explains, "They rebuilt the junior high a couple years after the tragedy and a new group of students were enrolled. But the legend of the girl with the barbed wire hair changed after that. Instead of being about the ghost who haunted the alleyway behind the old fire house, it was all about her haunting you. Students there said that they sometimes saw Akiko following around a senior high student around town or as he walked home from school. They'd seen her hugging you as you walked, placing her hand on your back, curling a strand of barbed wire to your neck like she had you on a leash. The students were both excited and terrified of the legend. And the stories only got more extravagant after you left town, even though nobody ever saw you or the ghost again."

When Yusuke hears this, his heart sinks in his chest. He had no idea this was still going on. He hoped that Akiko's soul had been freed and she was finally able to rest. He had no idea she was still with him, invisible to him.

Yusuke lowers his eyes. He doesn't know what to say.

"I guess that means she's here with us right now, huh?"

Narumi busts into laughter. "Kind of spooky, isn't it? Maybe it would have been better if you didn't know..."

Yusuke agrees with her. He has no idea how he's going to go on knowing that Akiko's always there beside him. He has no idea how he'll even be able to sleep at night or change his clothes or take showers without imagining her with him at all times, staring at him with her sunken eyes and snake-like metal hair.

"At least you'll never be alone," she says, lowering her eyes as though she knows full well how lonely life can be without somebody to share it with.

They talk for a while longer, reminiscing. Narumi fills him in on what happened to some of the kids from their school. She mentions how Itachi is in jail for selling drugs and how Touma ended up being pretty successful and respected even though he was a despicable hoodlum when he was young. He now runs a successful chain of ikayaki shops and is married with three kids. Hiroto works as a contractor with his father and is a miserable piece of shit that nobody wants anything to do with.

Once customers start filling up the coffee shop, Narumi says she has to go back to work and they say their goodbyes. They exchange phone numbers and Narumi says she'll text him the next time she's in the city. She makes him promise that he'll show her a fun night on the town, complaining that she hasn't had one of those in as long as she can remember. Yusuke agrees and they part ways.

Yusuke feels more empty than ever after the trip to his hometown. He can't stop thinking about the family he left behind, the people he used to know. But he especially can't stop thinking about Akiko. He now knows she's always there, always with him. He finds it difficult sleeping at night, imagining she crawls in bed with him as she did when he was young.

He can't concentrate at work, imagining her hovering over him, watching his every move. He's beginning to fall behind, beginning to lose the respect of his coworkers. His boss doesn't feel like he's as dependable as he was just last month and asks him what's wrong, but Yusuke has no way of explaining what is getting in the way of his work. He can't just tell him about how he found out he's being haunted by a ghost from his childhood. He knows that would only make things worse.

On his days off, Yusuke finds himself drinking a lot more than he used to. He goes to the bar a couple of blocks from his apartment and wastes his paycheck on expensive sake and overpriced ikura sushi with raw quail eggs. He always drinks heavily and always drinks alone, spending most of his time off recovering from hangovers.

But one night after two small bottles of sake and a few glasses of Sapporo, a woman comes over to him and asks to sit down. When Yusuke looks over at her, he can't believe how attractive she is. She's way out of his league. Five years younger, wearing a small blue dress, her long black hair styled like she works as a model. She pulls the bar stool close to him and stares him in the eyes.

"Umm… hello," Yusuke says to her, unable to look such an attractive woman in the eyes. "Was there something you needed?"

"I just want to spend some time with you," she says.

Yusuke doesn't know how to respond. He's never been approached by any woman in a bar before, especially not one like her. He's surprised she's even in such a trashy establishment. It's usually just old businessmen drinking here, just the saddest faces in the city. Not too many pretty girls come in who aren't escorts for some sleazy loser with a barcode hairstyle.

"I like how you look in that suit," she tells him, nodding toward his work clothes. "You look very handsome."

It seems like she's making fun of him. He wonders if somebody he worked with, maybe even his boss, paid this woman to come and flirt with him. It's the only thing that makes sense. Perhaps his boss thought he'd get his mojo back at work if Yusuke got laid so he hired some strange woman to show him a good time.

They don't talk much, but Yusuke has another drink with the woman. She just stares at him, leaning closer and closer.

When their drinks are finished, she says, "Bring me home with you. I want to be with you tonight."

Yusuke shrugs and accepts. He's been so lonely that the idea of being with a woman, especially one as beautiful as this girl, fills him with anticipation. Maybe his boss paid for her, maybe she actually finds him attractive, maybe she plans to just handcuff him to his bed and take him for everything he's worth. But whatever the case might be, he's going to go for it. If anything at least it will be a diversion from all the loneliness and monotony he's been suffering through for so long.

They go back to Yusuke's tiny apartment. He apologizes for the size, for the mess, but the woman doesn't seem to care. She grabs him and pulls him into the bed. She kisses him and tears his clothes off and makes love to him in such a furious way that he can't believe how lucky he is. Nobody's ever done that to him before. Nobody's ever wanted him so bad.

But then he starts thinking about Akiko. He realizes that she's still there, still watching him. She must be seeing this, witnessing him make love to another woman. She surely sees this as him cheating on her. Although she's not able to harm anyone who isn't a student at his old junior high, he can't help but think about what she wants to do to them. She'd probably wrap her barbed wire hair around this woman's neck and rip her head off. She'd probably want to make Yusuke's life a living hell for sleeping with another woman.

It almost makes Yusuke want to throw the woman off of him and apologize over and over again, hoping to save the woman's life. But before he can do anything, he finds himself bursting into orgasm. The woman cries out and comes with him. Then they fall into the bed, wrapping themselves around each other, hugging each other closely.

As they lie there, the woman kisses his cheek and ear and then curls into the crook of his neck. She closes her eyes and falls into sleep.

"That was nice," Yusuke tells her, not knowing what else to say. "Thank you."

But she's already asleep. Yusuke closes his own eyes and holds her in his arms, hoping that Akiko isn't watching them, praying that he didn't commit some kind of sin that will send her spirit back into a vengeful rage.

The next morning, Yusuke wakes to the woman screaming in bed next to him. He goes into a panic, looking over at her curled up against the wall, the blanket around her. He's sure Akiko is attacking her, trying to kill her for what she did, but Yusuke doesn't see anything wrong with her. She's not bleeding or wrapped in barbed wire. She's just terrified.

"What's wrong?" Yusuke cries. "Are you okay?"

He looks around for a sign of the ghost, but she's nowhere in the room. Then he realizes that woman isn't scared of some vengeful spirit. She's terrified of Yusuke.

"Who are you?" the woman cries. "How did I get here?"

Yusuke is shocked by her words. He has no idea what she's talking about.

He asks her, "What do you mean? You don't remember?"

She flinches when he tries to come close and shakes her head in response. Yusuke realizes that he's naked and that it's making her uncomfortable, but she has all of his bedding so he can't cover himself quickly. He goes for his clothes, hoping it will make the situation less awkward. She must have been trashed last night, so drunk she doesn't remember what she was doing. It kind of makes sense to him. It's the only way a woman that good-looking would ever be interested in sleeping with him.

"I'm sorry," he explains while pulling on his pants. "You asked me to bring you back to my apartment. You were the one who pulled me into bed."

"Liar!" the woman screams. "I would never do that. I'm engaged to be married. You must have drugged me, you nasty shit face!"

Yusuke shakes his head. He bows several times, trying to convince her that it's not the truth. He tries to hand the woman her clothes, but it only makes her more upset. When she sees her bra and underwear in his hand, she throws pillows at him, screaming at the tops of her lungs, calling him all manner of names while tears run down her cheeks.

Yusuke can't help but cry for her. He can't believe this has happened. He has no idea how it went so wrong.

He says, "I'm sorry. I don't know what else to say. Please believe me. I'm so sorry."

He kneels on the ground and bows until his forehead touches the floor. "I meant no offense. Please forgive me."

But the woman doesn't calm down. As Yusuke remains prostrated, the woman pulls on her clothes beneath the blanket. Then she gets off the bed, grabs her heels and smacks Yusuke on the back several times.

"You ruined my life, you bastard!" she cries, hitting him until she no longer has any strength to continue.

Yusuke takes it all. He feels terrible for her. If he knew she was so drunk that she was not in control of her senses, he never would have taken her home with him. He realizes what a horrible mistake he's made. He feels like the worst person in the whole world.

The woman grabs her purse and races out of the apartment, not bothering to even close the front door. Yusuke can hear her still screaming at him as she flees, waking up all the neighbors and causing them to come out to see what all the commotion is about. Yusuke steps out into the hallway and watches her leave. His neighbors glare at him for being responsible for such a commotion. They don't seem to even care about the girl, just upset that she caused such a disturbance.

The old guy next door eyes Yusuke down. Without saying a word, he tells him not to bring any trashy women around here ever again or else there's going to be consequences.

Yusuke spends the next couple of days terrified about what will happen to him. He finds it even more difficult to concentrate at work once he returns to the office. He's sure he's going to be arrested for raping that girl and he isn't sure whether it would be undeserved or not. If the police come he will accept all punishment with respectfulness. Even though he doesn't think he did anything wrong, he knows that it makes no difference in the eyes of the victim. The result is exactly the same as if he really did drug her and slept with her against her will. He's ready to go to jail if that's what it will take to let her rest easy.

But nothing ever happens. The police never come for him. The woman said she was engaged. She probably doesn't want to go to the police because she's worried about how it would affect her relationship with her fiancé. If he finds out about the encounter he might not want to marry her anymore. He might see her as having cheated on him. He might see her as damaged goods. It's a thing that happens way too much in the city. And while Yusuke is relieved that he won't be going to jail for what had happened, it only makes him feel more guilty that he got away with it. He feels terrible about how that woman will go through the rest of her life thinking a strange man took advantage of her.

A few nights later, another woman approaches him. She comes up to him on the street and stops him on the sidewalk.

She says, "Hi, how's it going?" as though they are familiar acquaintances.

Yusuke wonders if he knows her from somewhere, maybe from work. But based on her clothes, she's a tourist, probably been in town for less than a few days. She's also a Westerner with large breasts and long blond hair, but speaks perfect Japanese like she's lived here her whole life.

"I had a great time the other night," she says, stepping forward and touching his cheek. "It really made me happy to be with you again."

Her words send a chill down Yusuke's spine. He steps back from her, not sure what to make of what she's saying.

As Yusuke recoils from her, the woman stares at him with confused eyes. She's much taller than Yusuke, her big blue eyes looking into him with such familiarity.

"Don't you remember?" she asks. "We made love all night. It was such a beautiful experience. I've not been able to get it out of my mind."

She speaks to him as though she's the woman he slept with last week, the one who thought he'd drugged and raped.

"Bring me home with you," she says. "I want to be with you tonight."

They are the same words that the other woman said to him. When he looks more carefully, he sees more similarities. She looks at him the same way the other woman did. She has the same posture.

Yusuke's mouth drops open. He steps back, saying, "How is this possible? Who are you?"

She moves closer to him. "I'm the woman who loves you. I want to be with you. Always."

Yusuke whimpers as she reaches out to him, trying to grab him and kiss him.

"I need to feel you inside of me," she says.

But he dodges her and says, "Stay back."

Then he runs away. He can't bear the thought of doing the same thing as he did with the woman the night before. He can't wake up the next day to a woman who thinks she's been molested by a strange man. He can't possibly sleep with another woman ever again.

The woman runs after him, but isn't able to keep up for long. Yusuke keeps running until he realizes he's no longer being followed and then turns around and watches her from a distance. He sees the woman quiver a little, shaking like she's having a brief seizure on her feet, and then she looks around as though she has no idea where she is or what she's doing. Then she walks away.

Yusuke is pretty sure he knows what's going on. He doesn't know how it can be true, but it's the only thing that makes sense. Akiko has somehow learned how to possess other women's bodies.

The next day, things get really out of hand. As Yusuke's walking to the subway station on his way to work, strange women keep approaching him.

A young woman in a white skirt comes up to him and says, "I'm sorry about last night. Did I offend you or something?"

He ignores her and keeps moving.

Another woman, one with short hair and business clothes, jumps in his path and says, "I'm sorry if I made you mad. What can I do to make it better?"

He rushes past her, but soon an older woman with red hair dye comes by his side, walking backward as she speaks.

"I want us to spend more time together," she says. "I want it to be like it was before. I need to feel your body against mine."

But Yusuke doesn't even look her in the eyes. He enters a crowd of people, pushing his way through, keeping away from the woman as she calls out his name.

When he gets to the subway platform, a young senior high school girl in pigtails and bright pink lipstick grabs him by the arm and says, "I just want to be with you. What's wrong with that? Don't you love me?"

She won't let him go, holding as tight as she can. When other people around him see what's going on, they all give him horrible looks, silently judging him like he's in an inappropriate relationship with a minor. But none of them do anything about it, despite how bad it looks.

"You're my soulmate!" the school girl cries. "I want to be with you forever! I'm finally able to touch you again! Let me be with you!"

Yusuke tries to pull his arm out of her grasp, having an anxiety attack with all of the eyes watching them, but she won't let go.

He tells her, "You can't use women's bodies like this. It's not right. You need to stop it."

"But I love you!" the school girl screams at the tops of her lungs, bringing all attention to them. "I must be with you! I won't rest until we're together!"

Yusuke looks her in the eyes, looking past the school girl being possessed and into Akiko's soul. He says in a firm tone, "We can't be together. You're dead and I'm alive. What we had together ended years ago."

But this doesn't go over very well. The girl's eyes grow wide. She becomes angry.

"I'll kill them without you," she says, her voice growing deeper. "I'll kill all of them."

"Kill who?" he asks. "What are you talking about?"

The girl's eyes become dark and hollow. Her voice becomes demonic. She says, "I'll kill everyone at school. Every one of them I find. I'll kill everyone who gets between us. I'll kill everyone you meet."

The girl lets go of Yusuke and runs toward the tracks. She screams as she charges forward. She leaps into the air, aiming for an oncoming train, trying to kill the young girl she's possessing. But a large man rescues her. He jumps forward and grabs her, then pushes her back to the ground, asking her what the hell is wrong with her.

Within a moment, the girl comes to her senses. She has no idea what she's doing or why some strange man is holding her to the ground. Akiko has left her body.

Yusuke doesn't make eye contact as he gets onto the subway, especially not the teenage girl who had been yelling at him while she was possessed. The other people on the train might be glaring at him, disturbed that he would carelessly bring a young girl to suicide by rejecting her in such a harsh manner, but he just ignores them all. He's too disturbed by what Akiko said to him. He's terrified that the tragedy that happened ten years ago is going to happen again. And just like last time, it will be all his fault.

CHAPTER
EIGHT

Weeks go by, then months. He watches the news closely, waiting for something to happen to students at his old junior high. But there are no reports of any students dying or going missing. He doesn't run into any strange women wanting to sleep with him. He just keeps his head down and tries to do a good job at his work, thinking it would be better not to interact too closely with anyone. He's terrified of what would happen if Akiko possesses someone again and threatens to kill them if he doesn't give her affection. If that were to happen he's not sure what he'd do. He couldn't sleep with her in another person's body, but he couldn't anger her to the point that she murders the person whose body she's possessing. He'd have to make a compromise. He'd have to spend time with her, maybe hug her or hold her hand, without doing anything that would be disrespectful to the body Akiko was using.

When enough time passes, Yusuke realizes that Akiko is gone for good. He's sure that she must have realized that they could never be together and moved on. Maybe she went back to the alleyway behind the old fire station in his hometown. Maybe she found somebody else to haunt. But if she was still with him she would have done something by now. She would have possessed another woman to communicate with him. She would have killed someone out of spite or done something horrible that he can't even imagine. But there's been nothing. It's like she's no longer with him at all.

Narumi contacts Yusuke out of the blue one day. She says she's coming to the city and wants to hang out, reminds him that he promised to show her a good time. At first, Yusuke's worried about seeing her. He almost refuses. If Akiko is still around she might possess Narumi's body and force her to kill herself right in front of him, as punishment for rejecting her. But it's been quite a while since Akiko made that threat and nothing's happened. It's also been a long time since Yusuke has been able to socialize with anyone he doesn't work with and has been growing rather lonely. He'd love to see Narumi again, even if it's just for one night.

When he meets her outside of a Wagyu steakhouse that he picked out, Yusuke is surprised to see Narumi wearing such a beautiful dress with her hair made up like she just spent a ton of money at an upscale hair salon. Although he is wearing his best clothes and made himself look as presentable as possible, he wasn't expecting much from Narumi. He didn't think she would dress up like they were going on a fancy date.

"Hi, Narumi," Yusuke says when he meets her.

She turns to him and smiles. "So you finally showed up, Zombie-chan. I thought you were going to stand me up."

He wonders if he should compliment her on her hair and outfit, but instead, he finds himself bowing and apologizing for being late. He's not sure if it's a date or not. For all he knows, she's dressed up because she's meeting another guy after this. He doesn't want to embarrass himself.

"You're buying, right?" she asks him.

Yusuke nods and says, "Yeah, get anything you want."

She smiles and replies, "Good. I plan to."

Narumi blows through Yusuke's budget in ten minutes flat, ordering the best cut of steak and most expensive bottle of wine. But she does so with such enthusiasm that Yusuke can't help but let her get away with it. As long as she's happy, it's worth the money. He hasn't had a good night out with a friend in so long that it's worth it no matter how much it costs.

"I'm sorry for how I was back in junior high," Narumi says to him as a waiter pours her a glass of wine. "I was kind of a bitch back then."

Yusuke is surprised she would admit this, but accepts her apology. He says, "You were the only one who helped me back then. I owe you everything for that."

Narumi burst into laughter. "I handcuffed you to a fire pole and filmed you being raped by a ghost. I was a total nightmare."

Yusuke looks down. He completely forgot she had done that, forgot how betrayed he felt in that moment. But for some reason, he doesn't want her to feel guilty.

He says, "It doesn't matter. You were the one who saved me in the end, so I forgive you."

Narumi nearly blows wine through her nostrils. "But I showed that tape to everyone in school. I was terrible. Everyone saw you naked with Akiko. They saw you get wrapped up in her barbed wire as she had her way with you."

Yusuke breaks eye contact. He never knew that other people in school were aware of what happened. He had no idea that she kept all video evidence of that day.

Narumi continues, "I deleted the video, if you were wondering. After I left junior high, I wasn't able to see Akiko in the recording. It was just footage of you naked, tied to a pole. You were clearly being groped by something, lifted off the ground, kissing something that wasn't there. It was too awkward to hold onto, so I got rid of it."

She takes a swig of wine and says, "Anyway, I'm sorry for having recorded it at all. You didn't deserve that."

Yusuke just shrugs it off and smiles. He says, "Let's not talk about any of that. It's all in the past."

Narumi's face beams with excitement.

She says, "Yeah, fuck the past!" She raises her glass of wine. "Here's to the future!" It causes such a disruption in the restaurant that many of the customers look over at them with annoyance.

Yusuke returns his eyes to hers and raises his glass with her. They eat dinner and talk about what they wish they could do with their lives. Narumi talks about how she wants to move away from town and into the city. She asks if she could move in with Yusuke until she finds her own place and he agrees. She says she's dying to start her life over, that she feels like she's already getting old and her life has never even started yet. Yusuke promises to do whatever he can for her. Even if his apartment is small, he says she can stay for as long as she wants.

Yusuke and Narumi spend the whole night together, exploring all the interesting parts of the city. They visit the Studio Ghibli museum just before closing, they watch people cartwheel across Shibuya Crossing, they rent a room to do karaoke and sing lame songs they remember from their childhood, and then hit a 24-hour maid café where they drink coffee and have dessert. Narumi is especially interested in going to the maid café because everyone always said that's where she'd end up working as an adult and she always wanted to see one in person. She even applied for a job there and they said they might call her back for an interview.

When they get back to Yusuke's apartment, he can't believe how exhausting the whole night was. But he's more surprised by how much energy Narumi still has. She stopped by the corner store and grabbed a mountain of snacks and alcohol, like she's ready to keep going well into the morning.

"You're so lucky living in the city," Narumi says. "This is so much more fun than back home. I'm having the time of my life."

She busts into her snacks and spreads them across the hardwood floor, picking through the ones she finds most appealing. She takes a chug from a twenty-four-ounce can of beer and then stuffs a handful of pineapple candy in her mouth.

Yusuke sits on his bed, just watching the girl enjoy herself on his apartment floor. He can't believe she's there with him. The most beautiful girl in his hometown is actually having the time of her life in front of him.

Almost as though she can read his mind, Narumi says, "I don't know what it is about you, but I've always been happy when I'm in your company. I think there's just something exciting about you that you don't even notice yourself. It makes you unintentionally cool, which is way better than being naturally cool."

Yusuke shakes his head. He has no idea what she's talking about.

"I always longed to have a supernatural experience, and then I meet you who attracts a ghost girlfriend like it's nothing to you. I wish more than anything to move to the city and you live here like it's the most normal place to be in the world."

Yusuke has no idea what to say about that. It's not like he asked for any of those things. He was nice to a helpless homeless girl he met in an alleyway and she fell in love with him. He moved to the city because his parents ran him out of town. Neither of those things ever made him feel special. They only haunted him.

"I always have the best time with you." Narumi lies down on the hardwood floor and leans her head against a dresser, holding a beer between her breasts. "I wish every day was like this. My life sucks back home. I still live with my parents. My job is boring and pays shit. Most of my friends got married, had kids, and moved away." She looks over at Yusuke. "Would it really be okay if I move in with you? I wasn't joking. If I get a job at that maid café I can share the rent. I can also cook and clean. I won't be a bother."

Yusuke can tell that the look in her eyes is serious, but he can't believe anyone would want to move in with him.

"But my place is so small," he tells her. "You'd actually feel comfortable here?"

Narumi shrugs. "It's fine for now. Once I have an income we can get a bigger place. I don't mind sharing a bed for a while if it's okay with you."

"What about your stuff?" Yusuke asks.

"I'll get it later. All I need is my clothes. I'm sure you have enough room for that." She rolls over on her stomach and looks at him with a coy smile on her face. "I'll make it fun for you, I promise."

Yusuke thinks about it for a moment. He realizes that he's not hesitating because he doesn't want her there. He's hesitating because of Akiko. He decides to tell Narumi all about what has happened to him since he saw her last. He tells her about the women that Akiko has been possessing, about the one he slept with, about the one who almost threw herself in front of a train because he rejected her.

But Narumi isn't in the least bit worried about it. She seems to be excited by the story, as though it is the most interesting thing she's heard in ages.

"That's fine with me," Narumi says. She gets on her knees and looks up at him. "I don't mind if Akiko possesses me. If you two want to be together, then I won't stand in your way. You can use my body."

Yusuke is horrified by what she's saying. "You can't possibly mean that."

Narumi snickers. "I find it kinky and kind of exhilarating. I'd love it if something like that happened to me." She crawls up the side of his bed and looks him in the eyes. "It's so much more interesting than the boring relationships I've been in over the years. I'd definitely like to try it if it's possible."

Yusuke can't believe she's saying that. He thinks she has to be joking.

She gets to her feet and pulls off her shirt, exposing a black lace bra. "You wouldn't mind having sex with me, would you? You find me attractive, don't you?"

Yusuke doesn't answer her questions. It's obvious that he thinks she's beautiful. He's always thought she was. Even though it was Akiko who loved him, it was Narumi that he wanted more than anyone else in the world.

As Narumi takes off her bra and crawls into bed with Yusuke, she calls out to the emptiness of the room, "You hear that, Akiko? I give you permission to possess my body."

She pulls off her pants and exposes her naked flesh to Yusuke, sensually rubbing herself, trying to seduce him.

"You better do it quickly," Narumi tells the room. "Because I'm going to make love to your man either way."

Before Yusuke knows it, Narumi is pulling off his clothes and pulling him under the blankets with her. She makes love to him in a way he's never experienced before. She pulls him on top of her and bites into his neck, clawing into his back and fucking him in such a primal way that it doesn't take him long to have an orgasm. When he finishes, she straddles his face and forces him to give her oral sex until she tightens her thighs against his neck and squirts what feels like a gallon of warm fluid all over him, splashing across his face and neck, draining down his throat. It tastes a lot like urine, like Narumi just pissed on him. He doesn't complain about it. If that's the case, he's sure she didn't do it on purpose.

It's both the best and strangest sex he's ever had. As Narumi lies down and gets comfortable next to him, she uses her naked butt to push him away, forcing him to the edge of the bed to give her more room. With the light still on, she falls asleep almost immediately, filling the room with her snores.

Even though she didn't say a thing while they made love, Yusuke can tell that it was Narumi the whole time. Akiko never came. She never possessed Narumi's body. Even though she was invited, Akiko didn't seem to want to take Narumi up on her offer.

For the next several days, Yusuke and Narumi spend as much time as possible together, exploring the city, doing fun and exciting things that Yusuke never even thought of doing before. They run naked through Shibuya Center. They stay in a capsule hotel and make loud noises as though they're having sex until they upset all the other people staying there and get kicked out. They go to a bathhouse and peek over the wall at each other. They dress up in full-sized tuna costumes and run through Tsukiji fish market pretending to save their tuna brethren from being sold into sashimi. It makes Yusuke feel like he's a kid again, like they're junior high kids who are just trying to make trouble. It's the first time Yusuke's actually felt like he was alive. He feels like he might be able to move on from his traumatic past.

Every night they make love and every night Narumi calls out to Akiko to take over her body, but Akiko never comes. Narumi seems to get off on pretending that she's being possessed by Akiko and tries to act like her and fuck him in a way that she thinks a ghost would have sex. Even though Yusuke goes along with it, he can tell that it's not Akiko that he's sleeping with. He remembers how passionately the girl with the barbed wire hair kissed him, how she looked him in the eyes when they made love. Narumi can't mimic that. Deep down, he knows she doesn't love him as much as Akiko did.

They move into a bigger apartment, much bigger than the last one. It's far too much than Yusuke can afford, but

Narumi was so in love with the place when they first saw it that he couldn't refuse. He just has to put in more hours at work, try harder for a promotion, and everything will work out. Narumi is so full of excitement every day that it encourages him to earn more. He wants her to be able to have everything she could possibly want. Everything has changed since she came into his life. Everything has been better. He can't possibly imagine being without her.

But despite all the fun he's been having with Narumi, he can't help but think about Akiko. Even though she was a monster, she was still his first love. She still loved him more than anyone he's ever known in his life. He longs to be loved like that again. He wants somebody who would do anything, even kill another person, just to be by his side.

Yusuke sees Akiko again on the way home from work one day. He's carrying a bouquet of flowers to give to Narumi, a thing she requests from him at least once a month, though Yusuke knows that once a month really means once a week. He comes across a woman a little younger than him, standing in the middle of the sidewalk, staring him in the eyes.

It doesn't take long for him to realize who it really is. Even though she's an adult woman with shoulder-length hair, a tall nose and bangs that cover her eyebrows, Yusuke can see Akiko looking at him through those wide black eyes. He'd recognize them anywhere.

"I miss you," Akiko tells him, blocking his way home. "I never stop thinking about you."

Yusuke pauses in front of her. He lowers the flowers to his thigh, just in case she might think they are for her. He's not nervous around the possessed woman. He knows he should be terrified, but her posture shows that she doesn't mean any harm.

"I thought you were gone for good," Yusuke says.

She shakes her head. "I'll never leave you. I'll always be by your side." She steps forward to touch his cheek. "I love you."

Yusuke steps back before she can touch him and her hand falls to her side.

"I told you that we can never be together," Yusuke says. "If you wanted to make love to me then you could have possessed Narumi. She says she'll let you, any time you want. In fact, I'm pretty sure she wants you to."

Akiko shakes her head. "I don't want to just make love to you. I want to be with you always. I'll only use her body if I can take it over permanently. Would she agree to that?"

"No, I don't think so," Yusuke says. "Nobody would."

Akiko comes closer, her eyes wet and piercing into him. Even though she's in another body, Yusuke can't help but feel like he's gazing into the eyes of the real Akiko. She looks like she would have looked if she never died and grew to be the age of the woman whose body she's possessing right now. He has no idea how she found someone so similar in appearance. He wonders if she's even a niece or a younger sister or a lost relative.

"You know she could never love you like I do," Akiko says.

She goes to him and touches him, rubs her hand down his neck. Yusuke can't help but give in to her as she embraces him and kisses him gently on the cheek.

"You should be with me," she says. "I've been waiting an eternity for a love like yours. I can't handle not being with you."

Yusuke doesn't know what to say. He finds himself unable to resist as she pulls his face toward hers and kisses him deeply. When he closes his eyes, he feels like he did when he was in junior high, up in his bedroom, making out with Akiko when she was a ghost. But then he thinks of the girl's lips that he's kissing. They aren't Akiko's lips. They are some other woman's, some woman who hasn't given him permission to kiss her.

He pushes Akiko away. "I can't do it. Not in that body. Not without permission. If you want to kiss me you have to possess Narumi at a time when she agrees to let you."

Akiko steps away, an annoyed look on her face.

"I own this body now," Akiko says. "This woman gave it up. She doesn't want it anymore."

Yusuke looks at her, confused about what she's talking about. He doesn't know what she means until Akiko pulls down her sleeves and reveals the cuts on her wrists.

"She killed herself," Akiko explains. "She wanted to die and cut her wrists. She was bleeding out in her bathtub, seconds away from death when I took control of her body. Her spirit left and will never come back. This woman's life is mine now. I'm alive again and I want to spend my life with you."

She goes to him and wraps her arms around him. Yusuke hugs her back. He drops the bouquet on the ground and pulls her tightly to him. Even though he's in a relationship with Narumi, he can't help but be drawn to Akiko's arms. The warmth he feels is all-encompassing. He feels a love in her embrace that he's never felt from his mother, that he's never felt from Narumi. It's the love that he wants to feel more than anything in the world.

Akiko kisses him. She grabs his face with both hands and holds him in place so that she can suck his tongue into her mouth. Tears fall from her eyes and pool against his cheeks. Yusuke can't help but accept all of her love despite what she is, despite everything that's happened.

But Yusuke still finds himself pushing her away.

"I can't," he says.

Akiko's eyes go narrow. She steps back, fuming with anger.

"Why not?" she asks. "You want to be with that selfish bitch who's just using you? She only likes you because you saved her from her pathetic life. She doesn't love you. Nobody else will ever love you."

Yusuke looks away, becoming frightened by the woman. He knows she's not a normal human being. She's an onryo, a vengeful spirit. Despite how she looks, she's still the girl with the barbed wire hair who has killed so many people in the past.

"I'm sorry," Yusuke says. "It's just I can't be sure you're

not using the woman's body you're possessing against her will. You say she tried to kill herself, but that might not be true. You could have possessed her before that and cut her wrists on your own. You could be lying. I can't be sure."

Akiko bites her lip and tears roll down her cheeks. She becomes infuriated by his words.

"You don't believe me?" she cries. "You think I'm a liar?"

Yusuke shakes his head, trying to calm her down and not overreact. "That's not what I'm saying. I just don't feel comfortable with her body if I don't know for sure."

But this doesn't satisfy Akiko. She only becomes more enraged.

"You should love me no matter what!" she screams.

Her voice is so loud that anyone else on the street could hear it. Yusuke looks around, wondering if anyone is watching, but nobody else is here.

"You should love me even if I did steal this body!" Akiko continues. "You should be happy I went through all the trouble to take over another woman's life just so we can be together!"

Yusuke steps away from her. She's becoming so angry that she looks like she's about to kill somebody.

"I'm sorry, Akiko," he tells her. "I wish there was another way, but we just can't be together. Not like this." He picks the flowers up from the sidewalk. "I'm going home to Narumi."

As Yusuke turns to walk away, Akiko screams at the top of her lungs. It's a horrific, inhumane scream. Then she falls to the ground, begging Yusuke to come back to her. She slams her head on the pavement over and over, crying for him to be with her. He keeps moving. When he's a good distance away, he looks back to see her hitting her head so hard that the skin on her forehead breaks open, blood splashes across the sidewalk. Once her skull cracks and her brains fall out, the body she's possessing goes limp and falls over.

Whether Akiko got the body from a girl who wanted to die or not, she's dead for good now. She won't be coming back.

When Yusuke gets home, he tells Narumi everything that happened with Akiko, even the part about him kissing her, even the part where he said he would be with her if she used Narumi's body instead of the strange women she was possessing. Instead of being upset, Narumi becomes thrilled by his story. She can't believe something so crazy happened to him on the way from work, especially the part where Akiko bashed her own head in on the concrete.

Narumi makes love to him more passionately than she had in months, biting his ears and neck as hard as she can as she comes on him, flooding him with warm fluids, soaking the sheets and blanket.

When they're finished, Narumi lies next to him and says, "You know I'm willing to share if you both want, right? She said she didn't want to possess me if it was only for sex, but I'd be willing to let her have my body on Mondays and Wednesdays. It's a good compromise if you ask me. You could still be together if you wanted. Two days a week, she could be all yours."

Yusuke thinks about it for a minute. He doesn't say anything, though. He's not sure if it's a test, if Narumi is just wondering if he cares more about Akiko than he does her. But the idea of having both of them appeals to him. Feeling Akiko's love from within Narumi's perfect body seems like everything Yusuke could ever hope for.

But after thinking it over, Yusuke changes his mind.

"No, it's fine," he tells Narumi.

She's confused by his words. "What? You don't want to use my body to consummate your love with your ghostly sweetheart? You wouldn't be cheating. I think it would be hot."

Yusuke shakes his head. "Even if that's what she wants, I don't want to do it. I'd rather be with you."

Narumi laughs so loud it shakes the bed. "What the hell are you talking about? I'm just a temporary fling. You belong to her. You always will."

Yusuke thinks about it. For the first time in years, he thinks about what he wants, who he really wants to be with. Akiko is not that person. He doesn't even know her. Even if she kisses him in a way that he's never felt with Narumi, even if she's made love to him in a way that nobody else ever could, he doesn't really know anything about her. He couldn't imagine it would actually mean anything to him to be with her, even if she was in a human body, even if she possessed Narumi for two days a week.

Akiko's just a crazy, angry spirit. He couldn't imagine a life with her would be worthwhile. He couldn't imagine it would be nearly as fun and exciting as it is with Narumi. He can only imagine it as an endless nightmare with only a few sweet moments sprinkled here and there.

Being with Narumi is also sweet and also a nightmare, but what makes her a nightmare is kind of what makes Yusuke like her so much. She's never boring, she gives him a reason to work hard and bring home presents to make her happy. She makes him feel like he's got fire running in his veins whenever he's near her. If Akiko is a demon from hell, Narumi is a hell that brings out the demon in him. If he has to choose, it's Narumi that he wants to be with.

"No, I belong to you," Yusuke tells Narumi. "I always have. Tonight I realized that the only reason I loved Akiko is because it made you think I was special. Every time I kissed her or made love to her or had anything to do with her, I told you about it and it brought a smile to your face. It made you happy. It made you like me more."

Yusuke looks at her and continues, "If you want me to have sex with Akiko in your body, I will. But you should know that I wouldn't do it for my sake. I would only do it because you seem so excited for it to happen. I'd only do it so that you'll like me more. But other than that, I don't care. I don't want Akiko. I want you."

Narumi stares at him for a moment, then looks away. She lets out a long deep breath, almost like she's annoyed by everything he just said, as though he ruined everything by saying that.

She gets out of bed and goes to the bathroom. Yusuke watches her naked body, admiring her perfect ass as though it's probably the last time he'll ever get a chance to see it. He realizes he said the worst thing he possibly could. He realizes that she has no interest in a guy who obsesses over her like all the other guys always did. The thing that made her like him, the thing that separated him from everyone else, was that he was having a love affair with some deadly supernatural creature. She saw herself as the other woman in a weird paranormal love triangle and she liked it that way.

Narumi spends a very long time in the bathroom. She takes a long dump and an even longer shower. When she comes out, she's standing naked and dripping wet in the middle of the bedroom as though she didn't bother drying herself, staring at him with the most annoyed expression she's ever given him, Yusuke is sure she's about to dump him right then and there. But despite the expression on her face, that's not what she does.

"Okay, then," she says. "Fuck Akiko. You belong to me now."

Yusuke is shocked by her words. He wasn't expecting her to say that in the slightest.

She crawls back into bed with him. She wraps her arm tightly around his neck and hugs him close. Her breast nearly suffocating him as it presses against his mouth and nose.

"But if you're mine, that means you can never see Akiko ever again. If you ever sleep with her or kiss her, even if she possesses my body, then I'll murder you."

She releases Yusuke from her grasp, giving him space to breathe, and looks him in the eyes.

She says, "I'll kill you and send you to her and you'll spend the rest of eternity together whether you like it or not."

Then Narumi steps out of bed and looks around the room, trying to find an invisible woman who might be there, somewhere.

"Do you hear that, Akiko?" she cries, her voice echoing through the empty room. "If he wants you then I'll send him to you. But until then, he's mine. Don't get in my way."

She says this in such a threatening way that Yusuke realizes that Narumi is actually far more terrifying than Akiko when she wants to be. If the girl with the barbed wire hair was listening, she'll surely think twice before crossing her.

CHAPTER
NINE

After another year of dating, Narumi and Yusuke get married. They have the ceremony in the city with quite a large number of people in attendance. It's mostly Yusuke's boss and coworkers, who felt obligated to attend, as well as Narumi's family and a whole lot of her friends from back home.

Yusuke isn't sure but he swears that he hears all of Narumi's friends making fun of her for marrying Zombie-chan, a couple of them even seemed offended and angry about it because they had friends who died in the tragedy that took place back when they were kids, the one they think Yusuke was responsible for. But Yusuke relaxes once he realizes that their criticisms only make Narumi happier. She relishes the thought of marrying the guy who seduced the girl with the barbed wire hair. It almost seems like the only reason she invited them to the wedding was to see how shocked they would be by who she was marrying.

Even though he doesn't realize until the ceremony is over, Yusuke's mother is also in attendance. They sent her an invitation but she never gave a response. She never congratulated them or gave them a gift or said a single word during the reception. But she was there, in the back of the room, watching her son during the happiest moment of his life. When it's all over, Yusuke doesn't approach her, even though he wants to. He desperately would like to speak to her again. He wants her to say that she still loves him. He wants her to apologize for turning her back on him. But she doesn't do anything but sit in the back of the room with a dead expression on her face. And the second she notices Yusuke looking over at her, she just gets up and walks out, trying not to get in the way of all the happiness emanating around her.

But Yusuke's mother does come back into his life again, after her first grandchild is born. Narumi gives birth to a daughter that they name Sora and she is the most beautiful little girl that either of them have ever seen. They both fall instantly in love with her. When Yusuke sends a photo to his mother, she falls in love with the child more than anyone. It's like everything is forgotten in the blink of an eye.

Yusuke's mother shows up at their door one day, desperate to see her granddaughter. They now live in a much nicer place, a house in the Hatagaya suburb that is Narumi's pride and joy. After Yusuke's promotion to executive of marketing, he's been making enough money to provide his family with a very comfortable way of life. His wife and daughter will never have to worry about financial hardship ever again. But in less than a year, Narumi has already grown into a snobbish suburban wife. When she sees Yusuke's mother at the door, she glares down at her like some vagrant is begging for change.

"What makes you think you can see my baby?" Narumi tells her, more disgust on her face than Yusuke has ever seen. "You turned your back on your son. What makes you think you're welcome in this household?"

Yusuke's mother bows several times, prostrating herself to the daughter-in-law she knows next to nothing about.

"I'm very sorry for my behavior," the old woman says, holding her head down. "Please let me see my granddaughter."

But her behavior only makes Narumi laugh at her like she's the most pathetic person in the world.

"I don't think so," Narumi says. "You knew everything that happened to Yusuke is your fault and yet you let him take the blame. Your son is the sweetest man I've ever known and you threw him away like garbage to protect your reputation in a shithole of a town. You're never going to see my daughter for as long as you live."

Yusuke's mother continues bowing and apologizing, begging for her mercy.

Narumi leans in, speaking right into her ear in the nastiest voice she can muster. "If you want to see her then just kill yourself and come back as a ghost like your old friend, Akiko—the one you probably killed yourself. That's the only way you're getting past me to see her."

Yusuke witnesses the whole occurrence from the living room. Even though he's bitter toward his mother, even though he loves seeing his wife tear her apart and say all the things he wishes he could say to her, he can't just let her leave. As his mother apologizes for the last time and turns to go, Yusuke goes to the door and calls her inside. Narumi objects but Yusuke says it's fine.

"You can at least see her once," he tells his mother.

A smile appears on the old woman's face, but she doesn't thank Yusuke. She doesn't look him in the eyes or say a single word to him. She just pushes past him to get inside, demanding to see the baby.

Narumi is full of vitriol when she leads the woman to the child's room. She glares at Yusuke, annoyed that he let that horrible person lay eyes on their perfect, beautiful child. But she brings the mother to the room anyway, hoping to get it over with as soon as possible.

When Yusuke's mother sees the baby, she looks at it with confusion. She looks up at Narumi and then back at the child, like she doesn't recognize it from the photograph.

"This isn't right," she tells them.

Yusuke's mother backs away from the crib, horrified by the sight of the child.

"What's wrong?" Yusuke asks.

His mother finally looks him in the eyes. She gives him such a frightened, angry look.

"Your child is wrong," she says, her voice growing deep. "She's cursed."

Narumi freaks out when she hears the woman's

words. She can't believe the old hag would say something so horrible.

"What the fuck?" Narumi cries. "You wanted to see my baby and you say she's cursed?"

Yusuke's mother looks down at the child. She looks at it as though she sees something that nobody else sees.

"She's not right," says Yusuke's mother. "You have to get rid of her. If she lives she'll bring nothing but darkness on this world."

When she says this, Narumi loses it. She shoves Yusuke's mother against the wall and yells, "How dare you say such a thing about her! Get the fuck out of my house!" She pushes the old woman out of the room, shoving her in the direction of the exit. The baby starts crying and Yusuke picks her up in his arms, cradling Sora with love, trying to calm her down.

Narumi cries, "Never come back! You're not welcome here!"

Yusuke's mother doesn't resist. She moves as fast as she can to get out of the house. But when she's at the doorway, she turns back and says, "Please, listen to me. That thing is cursed. She's not human. You can't let her live."

As she says this, she still doesn't look at Yusuke. She only pleads to Narumi. She acts like he doesn't matter, that he's not even a person to her anymore. Because of this, Yusuke is the one who goes to his mother and shoves her out the door. Before she can say another word to his wife, Yusuke slams the door in her face. Like Narumi, he'll never let his mother ever show her face in his house ever again.

"She's lost it," Yusuke explains to his wife after his mother has left, handing Sora over to her. "She doesn't know what she's saying."

Narumi cradles her daughter, holding her baby lovingly in her arms, trying to protect her from that woman's nasty words.

"Well, she seemed convinced," Narumi says.

Yusuke explains, "She probably hasn't been mentally well for a long time. After what happened when we were young, what happened to the school, she probably has convinced herself that I'm evil. She probably thinks she's cursed for her part in Akiko's death. She probably thinks I was cursed because I'm her son and attracted the attention of a vengeful spirit. And so now she thinks my daughter is cursed as well and the horror will continue. It's all a delusion, probably brought on by her own guilt. Just forget about her."

After he finishes, Sora begins to cry again and Narumi opens her shirt to breastfeed the girl. She sits down next to Yusuke and looks him in the eyes.

"I'm going to ask you this just once," she says. "Tell me the truth."

Yusuke looks over at her. He can tell she's serious.

She asks, "When I became pregnant with Sora, was Akiko in control of my body?"

Yusuke is shocked by her words. He can't believe she'd say such a thing.

"Of course not!" Yusuke cries. "How could you think that?"

Narumi tries not to raise her voice while breastfeeding. She says, "I don't know. There's been plenty of times that we've had sex and I don't remember doing it. If Akiko took control of my body at the time that I got pregnant maybe our baby really is cursed."

Yusuke shakes his head. "The only times you don't remember were the times when you were drunk off your ass."

Narumi glares at him and raises her voice. "Are you calling me a drunk?"

Sora starts crying again, but Narumi just shoves her boob back in her mouth to shut her up.

Yusuke says, "No, but you almost always want to have sex when you drink and you sometimes don't remember what happened the next morning when you drink too much. Has there ever been a time that you've lost memory when you haven't been drinking at all?"

Narumi flares her nostrils and gets off the couch, cradling Sora tightly to her chest.

"If I find out you slept with Akiko and cursed our baby, you're going to suffer a fate way worse than death," she tells him. "I swear it. You'll wish I just killed you before it's over."

Yusuke has no idea what to say after that. He can't believe his mother's words affected her so much. For the next couple of days, Narumi barely speaks to him. She sleeps in the baby's room. She forgives him by the end of the week, but before that she acts as though he's been cheating on her. And because the woman he's been supposedly cheating on her with has been using her own body, she has no way of proving that it didn't happen. Whatever the case, Narumi tells him she's never getting blackout drunk ever again. She says if she ever wakes up without a memory of the night before, she'll know if he's been cheating. And if that ever happens he'll never see her or his daughter ever again.

The following years are both the best and worst of Yusuke's life. His relationship with Narumi has had its ups and downs. At times, Narumi is more passionate and loving than she's ever been. At others, she is a living nightmare who cares only about making every single second of Yusuke's life a constant and unending misery. She tortures him for having any kind of hobby or interest that isn't something that she thinks is worth his time. She gets angry when he doesn't do whatever he possibly can to make her happy, even things that she hasn't told him about yet. She wishes that he would revolve his life completely around her like he used to when they were first married.

It was the thing she liked best about marrying a man like Yusuke. He wasn't like that asshole Hiroto or other guys she dated. Because he worshipped her like a goddess, she could get away with anything. She could convince him to do whatever she wanted. He got so good at pleasing her that he started to know what she wanted before she even knew she wanted it. He showered her with gifts, her bought her all the clothes and furniture and jewelry she ever wanted. He provided her with the perfect life she always dreamed of. But he doesn't do enough for her anymore.

As Sora gets older, Yusuke has switched his priorities from making Narumi happy to providing for his family's needs, and this is not the kind of behavior Narumi finds acceptable in a husband. She wants to be spoiled again. She wants to be shown a crazy night out on the town from time to time. She's sick of being merely a housewife to the quiet nerdy kid she knew in school.

Although Narumi loves their daughter, she finds that she's not cut out to be a parent. She hates the constant responsibility and wishes she could go out and party. She wishes she had friends that weren't the wives of Yusuke's boring co-workers. She wants something crazy to happen to her, something as insane as when she first met Yusuke and got involved with the girl with the barbed wire hair. A part of her wishes Yusuke really would use her body to have an affair with Akiko. She would be pissed and maybe even leave him, but at least it would break up the monotony in her life. At least something exciting would actually happen to her.

Narumi has admitted all of this to Yusuke, hoping it would get some kind of reaction out of him. But he's so wrapped up in his work, so in love with spending time with his daughter, that he doesn't even humor her with a response. He tells her that he'll do whatever she wants. He just wants her to be happy.

"How the hell are you going to make me happy?" Narumi cries, sitting next to him in bed as he waves the sweat out of his underwear.

Yusuke grunts and snorts a cluster of mucus out of his nasal cavity.

"Why don't we take a family vacation next weekend?" he asks. "We can go to the beach. Sora's never seen the ocean before."

Narumi groans at the proposal. "That sounds so lame. I want to do something exciting."

Yusuke nods. "We can have your parents watch Sora and spend some time alone." He looks over at her and leans in to kiss her neck. "We can have a romantic night on the town." A goofy grin crosses his face. "Maybe even give Sora a little brother."

But what he says offends Narumi more than anything he could have proposed.

"You think I need another kid to be happy?" she cries. "I love Sora but there's no way in hell I'm letting you put another baby in me."

Yusuke gets the picture and moves back to his side of the bed. He pulls an old manga out of his nightstand and begins reading. Narumi doesn't mind interrupting him.

"Something interesting needs to happen or I'm going to go insane," she says. "I'm even more bored than I was when I was working at the coffee shop."

Yusuke puts down his manga. He looks over at his wife.

"What the hell's wrong with you?" he asks.

Narumi glares at him. He's never spoken to her like this before.

"It's like you're only happy when your classmates are

being ripped apart in front of your eyes," Yusuke says. "You miss the times when I'm being raped as a child in my bedroom or being wrapped in barbed wire around a fireman's pole that you handcuffed me to. Those weren't exciting memories to wish for again. They were horrific."

Narumi pauses for a moment. Then she freaks out on him. She's never heard him speak to her like that before.

"How could you say that?" she cries. "All I said is that our life isn't as exciting as it was when we were younger."

Yusuke sits up and lets out a long breath. Then he raises his voice, "There have been three times that I can remember where you've been at your happiest. One was the day we got married. Another was the day Sora was born. The third was the day you learned that Akiko broke some poor girl's head open against the pavement because I wouldn't sleep with her. If being married to me is boring to you now, if being Sora's mother is such a pain, I can only assume what you want is that murderous vengeful spirit back in our lives."

When Yusuke looks at his wife's face, he sees a look he's never seen before. She's more stunned and livid than she's ever been.

"I didn't say that at all!" Narumi cries. "How can you think that about me?"

Yusuke explains, "I'm sorry, but after what happened when we were young I've had enough excitement to last me a lifetime. I like boring. Boring is a luxury. I would love more than anything for our lives to stay exactly as it is, living in this nice house, raising our beautiful daughter. And believe it or not, being with you, even when we do nothing but sit together in silence or watch television or complain about how annoying the neighbors are, is enough to make me the happiest man on the planet. I don't need anything but this. I love our life the way it is."

When he's finished, Yusuke realizes how much of a mistake he made. He's never criticized Narumi before, not even for a second. Whenever she complains about being bored, which is pretty often, he's always bent over backward to make her happy. But not this time. He actually told her how he really feels.

He tries to backpedal by saying, "Tell me what would make you happy and I'll do it. I don't care what it is. I'll even run naked through Shibuya Center again, like we did before we were married, even if we get arrested. Anything you want. I promise."

But Narumi doesn't say anything. She just glares at him until he climbs out of bed and leaves the room. He sleeps on the couch and uses a decorative cushion as a pillow. He can't believe he's such an idiot for saying all those things. Narumi's a goddess. She's not the type to fall comfortably into the position of a mother and a housewife. She needs time to adjust. It's been five years, but that's still not long enough. He knows that if he wants to keep her he's going to have to do his best to give her the life she wants, no matter how extravagant and inconvenient her desires might be.

The next day, Yusuke apologizes to Narumi before he goes off to work. He spends the next several months doing everything he can to make Narumi happy. He takes her on luxurious vacations, brings her to the best restaurants in the city, flies her to Berlin and London. His efforts work well for a while and even reignite that spark in her eyes that made him fall in love with her, but she always falls back into a pit of boredom. She always wants something more exciting to happen to her. It's like she builds up a tolerance to interesting experiences. Once she does something that makes her happy, she'll never be happy again until she can try something even better than that. Yusuke realizes that he can't keep it up forever. She's too spoiled. She wants more than he'll ever be able to give her.

It isn't long before Narumi wants to leave him. Yusuke's heart is shattered when she tells him that she's moving out. He can't believe she'd give up their whole lives together, that she'd leave her own daughter, just because she's grown bored with her life in the suburbs.

"I'm sorry, I just can't take it anymore," Narumi says, holding her luggage in her arms. "I do love you. I love Sora. I want to be the woman you both deserve. But I'm just not. If I don't go now my resentment will make you both miserable. You'll be happier without me."

Yusuke just stares at her with tears in his eyes. He tries to think of something to say to her, something to convince her to stay with them, but there's not a single word that comes to mind. It's like his whole world is about to walk out the door but he can't speak, he can't even move.

When Sora figures out what's going on, she goes to her mother and asks, "Where are you going, Mommy? Are you going on a vacation?"

It seems like Narumi was hoping to get out of there before she had to face her daughter. When she looks down at the little girl in her flower-print dress and tiny pigtails, she bursts into tears.

Narumi picks Sora up and holds her tightly. Yusuke assumes that she's going to lie to her daughter and tell her that she's right, she is going on a vacation. But then Yusuke realizes that this is Narumi, the woman who's never backed down from a difficult conversation in her life.

Narumi shakes her head and speaks to Sora in the most gentle voice possible.

"I'm sorry, my baby girl," she says. "I'm not going on vacation. I'm moving out."

"Moving where?" Sora asks, wrapping her arms around her mother's shoulders, completely unaware of what Narumi really means by her words.

"I don't know yet," Narumi says. "But I'm going far away and I'm never coming back. I'll never see you again."

Narumi continues explaining in complete detail until her daughter completely understands what she's talking about. When it sinks in, Sora bursts into tears, crying at the top of her lungs.

"Don't go!" Sora cries. "Please don't go, Mommy! Please!"

As his daughter cries, Yusuke loses it. He starts crying even louder than Sora, yelling at Narumi for making such a horrible decision. Asking her how she can do this to her daughter, how she can just cut herself from her life.

Narumi tries to push her daughter away, but the young girl only clutches tighter to her clothes.

"Please, Mommy!" Sora screams. "Please!"

The little girl becomes belligerent, slurring her words between her cries and snorts and sniffles.

Narumi glares into Yusuke's eyes and says, "Take her. Get her off of me."

Yusuke does as she says. If he didn't get Sora away he's worried that Narumi would have used force and thrown her daughter to the floor. But when Yusuke takes her, Sora falls right into his arms and hugs tightly to him. She grabs him in such a way that it feels like she's worried that both of her parents are going to leave her, that if she can't have her mother she will at least hold onto her father. When she grips onto his shirt, it feels as though she will never let him go no matter what. Yusuke hugs her close to him, covering her eyes from her mother as she collects all her things and opens the front door.

"It's not too late to change your mind," Yusuke tells her, holding his daughter tightly. "Even if you leave and start a new life without us. Even if you find the excitement you're looking for. We'll still be here. We'll still be waiting for you."

Before Narumi leaves, she bursts into laughter. It's the same old dismissive, condescending, hateful laugh she's always given anyone who speaks to her in a serious manner. Yusuke used to love her laugh, but now he realizes just how cold and horrible it always ways.

She says, "Don't hold your breath."

Then she walks out the door and doesn't look back.

An hour passes. Yusuke holds his daughter in his arms, comforting her as she cries herself to sleep, her emotions overwhelming her so much that she just passes out from exhaustion.

Yusuke knew it was coming, but he still can't believe Narumi would leave them. She has nowhere to go, no one else to go to. If she had been cheating on him with a wealthy more attractive man it would make perfect sense, but that wasn't the case at all. He assumes she'll just move back in with her parents, maybe go back to working at the coffee shop until she figures out something else to do with her life. He prays that she'll eventually realize what a mistake she's made, that she'll see what a great life she had with them, how much her family really loved her, and eventually come back. It's the only thought Yusuke can hold onto to keep himself sane.

But it doesn't take long at all before Narumi comes back. After a couple of hours, she just walks through the front door and tosses her luggage on the floor. She steps into the living room, staring Yusuke in the eyes.

"I thought you left," Yusuke says. He moves Sora off of his lap and onto the couch, trying not to wake her up. "Did you forget something?"

Narumi shakes her head. She's got a calm expression on her face, completely different from the one she had before. Yusuke wonders if the act of leaving was enough to give her a change of heart. Perhaps Sora's tears that are still soaking her shirt were enough to show her what a horrible mistake she was making.

"I'm sorry," Narumi says. "I'm not going anywhere."

Yusuke can't believe her words. He stands up and goes to her.

"Are you sure?" he asks.

Narumi nods.

"I'll never leave you," she says. "I'll always be by your side."

Then she lunges at him and hugs him tightly, holding him like she's never held him before.

When Sora wakes up, she sees her mother in the entryway and cries with excitement.

"Mommy!" she screams and runs to her.

Narumi picks Sora up and holds her in her arms and then nuzzles her nose against the girl's soft cheek.

"I don't want you to go, Mommy," Sora says, sniffling against her mother's chest.

Narumi smiles and says, "I'm not leaving, my sweetheart. I love you too much. I'll never leave you."

Then she pulls Yusuke closer and hugs them together, pushing her face into Yusuke's chest.

"I'll be the best mother and the best wife that either of you could ever imagine from now on. I'll spend every waking moment making you both feel loved and happy. I promise."

Yusuke isn't sure what made Narumi change her mind so much in such a short period of time, but he's happy to have her back. He's happy to see his daughter smile with relief and not have to go without her mother for even a single day.

It doesn't take long for Yusuke to realize that Akiko has possessed his wife's body. When they lie down in bed together that night, she can't keep her hands off of him. She hugs him close, tugging on him like she never wants to let him go, not even for a second. Narumi's never felt that way about him before. She's never been so desperate to feel him against her body.

"I want to hold you forever and ever," she tells him, placing her cheek against his heart. "I want to show you how much I love you."

Yusuke doesn't know what to do. He runs his fingers through her hair, wishing that the woman holding him was the woman he married. But the longer he spends with her, the more convinced that it's really a ghost possessing her body.

"We have such a beautiful girl," Narumi says. "Don't you think so?"

Yusuke agrees. "Of course she is."

Narumi looks up at him. "I want another one. I want a bunch more."

Yusuke freezes up when she says this. He doesn't know

how to respond. Knowing that it's not really his wife, he realizes that he can't possibly agree to such a thing. He knows that he has to convince her to give Narumi's body back. He can't possibly let her continue this way.

But before he can say a word, Narumi is pulling his clothes off. She strips naked and gets on top of him. As she looks him in the eyes, he doesn't see Narumi looking back at him at all. He only sees Akiko. But there's something different in her eyes than he ever saw when he was young. Her eyes aren't filled with loneliness and desperation anymore. They are filled with hopefulness and happiness. They are the most beautiful eyes Yusuke has ever seen before.

"I want to give you so many babies," Narumi says, kissing his chest and neck. "I want to give you all the babies in the world."

Although Yusuke finds these words incredibly disturbing, he doesn't stop Narumi from crawling on top of him and making love to him. She kisses him deeply and licks every inch of his body. When she puts him inside of her, it doesn't feel anything like the sex he's previously had with his wife. It's so tender and passionate. It's not the craziest sex, not the most furious, or even the best sex Yusuke has ever had in his life. But it is the most intimate. He's never felt so close to another human being in his life. He's never experienced anything so beautiful.

When it's over and they lie together and fall asleep in each other's arms, listening to each other's heartbeats pulsing as one, Yusuke feels a wave of comfort spread throughout his body. He's never felt such warmth from another person in his whole life.

When he wakes up in the morning, Yusuke finds Narumi in the living room playing with Sora in her pajamas, showing her daughter more attention than she's ever shown her before. The whole room is filled with giggling and merriment, like it's a holiday or some special occasion. Breakfast is being kept warm in the oven. Coffee is brewing on the stove.

Narumi's face lights up when she sees Yusuke. She goes to him and kisses him good morning. Her face is so bright with happiness that it just lights up the room. She tells him to get ready for breakfast and goes to the kitchen to fix them some plates. She has prepared rice omelettes for them, a dish Narumi never knew how to make before. It smells absolutely delicious.

As Yusuke goes to his daughter, he sees that she's been coloring in a coloring book and building with Legos. He sits down next to her, checking to make sure she's okay. He needs to make sure the woman possessing her mother isn't harming her. He needs to make sure his daughter will be safe.

But Sora tells him, "I like Mommy better this way. I hope she stays like this forever."

When they sit together and have breakfast, Yusuke can't help but appreciate how happy his family looks together. Both his wife and daughter smile at him in such a way that it fills his heart with more joy than he's felt in a very long time.

He knows that it's wrong letting Akiko take over

Narumi's life. He knows that one day Narumi will come back and want revenge for having her body taken over by another woman. But Yusuke has to look after his daughter. He has to think about his family. And if Akiko makes Sora happy, if she never leaves her and gives her all the love a daughter like her deserves, then he thinks he can live with it. He doesn't know if he feels too sorry for Narumi after trying to abandon her family.

Everyone has a duty in life, some kind of responsibility that they are expected to fill whether they want to do it or not. And when you turn your back on that responsibility, there's going to be someone else who steps up and takes your place. You can't complain when this happens. You can only regret that you weren't strong enough to fulfill that role yourself. You can only watch as your responsibility blossoms into something better than it would have had you never given up on it.

When Narumi's eyes meet Yusuke's across the table, she winks at him. She rubs her lower abdomen, indicating that she's already pregnant even though they only had sex once. But he knows that she's going to make love to him every single night until she's pregnant again. Even though he can see that Akiko loves his daughter with all her heart, he knows that she won't rest until she has a child of her own, a child that she gives birth to herself, even if it's not her body that she delivers it from. She has always wanted to be a mother, but that was robbed from her when she died far too young. It is now an opportunity to start over, as a new person, in a new life. Even if she has to take it from somebody who didn't appreciate having it anymore.

Yusuke thinks everything will be better from now on. He thinks that he can truly love his wife, even if she's not really Narumi anymore. He thinks his daughter will be far happier, be far more loved than she would if she was left without her mother.

But when he sees Narumi reach out to touch Sora, holding her daughter's hand so tight that the girl cries out in pain, Yusuke wonders if he might be making a horrible mistake.

"I've been wanting to meet you for so long," Narumi tells Sora, gripping the little girl's hand even tighter. "I've been thinking about you every day since I made you, watching you every moment you were awake. It's so good that we can finally touch."

Sora pulls her hand from her mother's grip, bursting into tears at the pain. Narumi just smiles at Sora and tells her that she doesn't hurt nearly as much as she's been hurting without her.

When Narumi looks back at Yusuke, she says, "I've finally got everything I've ever wanted. I have all the happiness in the world. And I'll have more." As she looks at Yusuke, her eyes widen. They grow so wide that they look like they'll bug out of her sockets. "I'll have so much more."

Yusuke can't tell if he's imagining it, but he swears that in the corners of his eyes he can see a great mass of barbed wire growing out of his wife's scalp. It grows so long that it covers her face and buries her chest and lap. It crawls across the breakfast table, it curls around his arms and legs, it twists around his daughter as she eats breakfast. It climbs the walls and slithers across the floor. It encompasses every inch of his household. But even though the barbed wire is cold and rusty and sharp, he can't help but feel comforted by its grasp.

When he blinks, the barbed wire is gone. He can move his hands freely and continues to eat his breakfast. He smiles up at his wife and she smiles back at him with her eyes.

But even though he can no longer see it, Yusuke still knows that the barbed wire is still there, everywhere, digging deeper and deeper into his home, creating roots that will never be able to be torn out ever again. And even though he's sure the barbed wire will cause irreversible damage over time, he knows that there's no way to pull it out anymore. He has to live with it, learn to love it exactly as it is. Because, if he doesn't, those roots will tear his whole family apart.

BONUS SECTION

This is the part of the book where we would have published an afterword by the author but he insisted on drawing a comic strip instead for reasons we don't quite understand.

Thanks for reading my newest book, *The Girl with the Barbed Wire Hair.* Wasn't it spooky?

It's me CM3!

just finished reading it

girl with the barbed wire hair

WHAT THE FUCK KIND  OF ENDING WAS THAT!!

You didn't like it?

How could he let Akiko take over his wife's body like that?

Ummm... What?

Narumi was kind of a bitch but she didn't deserve that! Letting a psycho ghost possess his wife's body for the rest of her life just because she was about to leave him? It just makes Yusuke seem like a total asshole!

You can't let your protagonist do something that horrible!

His children are going to be cursed! Akiko will go on a murder spree!

This is a terrible ending!

What are you talking about?

That's not what happened.

Did you think that Akiko actually possessed Narumi at the end?

Yeah... I mean...

Didn't she?

ABOUT THE AUTHOR

Carlton Mellick III is one of the leading authors of the bizarro fiction subgenre. Since 2001, his books have drawn an international cult following, despite the fact that they have been shunned by most libraries and chain bookstores.

He won the Wonderland Book Award for his novel, *Warrior Wolf Women of the Wasteland*, in 2009. His short fiction has appeared in *Vice Magazine, The Year's Best Fantasy and Horror #16, The Magazine of Bizarro Fiction,* and *Zombies: Encounters with the Hungry Dead*, among others. He is also a graduate of Clarion West, where he studied under the likes of Chuck Palahniuk, Connie Willis, and Cory Doctorow.

He lives in Portland, OR, the bizarro fiction mecca.

Visit him online at **www.carltonmellick.com**

STACKING DOLL

Benjamin never thought he'd ever fall in love with anyone, let alone a Matryoshkan, but from the moment he met Ynaria he knew she was the only one for him. Although relationships between humans and Matryoshkans are practically unheard of, the two are determined to get married despite objections from their friends and family. After meeting Ynaria's strict conservative parents, it becomes clear to Benjamin that the only way they will approve of their union is if they undergo The Trial—a matryoshkan wedding tradition where couples lock themselves in a house for several days in order to introduce each other to all of the people living inside of them.

SNUGGLE CLUB

After the death of his wife, Ray Parker decides to get involved with the local "cuddle party" community in order to once again feel the closeness of another human being. Although he's sure it will be a strange and awkward experience, he's determined to give anything a try if it will help him overcome his crippling loneliness. But he has no idea just how unsettling of an experience it will be until it's far too late to escape.

MOUSE TRAP

It's the last school trip young Emily will ever get to go on. Not because it's the end of the school year, but because the world is coming to an end. Teachers, parents, and other students have been slowly dying off over the past several months, killed in mysterious traps that have been appearing across the countryside. Nobody knows where the traps come from or who put them there, but they seem to be designed to exterminate the entirety of the human race.

Emily thought it was going to be an ordinary trip to the local amusement park, but what was supposed to be a normal afternoon of bumper cars and roller coasters has turned into a fight for survival after their teacher is horrifically killed in front of them, leaving the small children to fend for themselves in a life or death game of mouse and mouse trap.

NEVERDAY

Karl Lybeck has been repeating the same day over and over again, in a constant loop, for what feels like a thousand years. He thought he was the only person trapped in this eternal hell until he meets a young woman named January who is trapped in the same loop that Karl's been stuck within for so many centuries. But it turns out that Karl and January aren't alone. In fact, the majority of the population has been repeating the same day just as they have been. And society has mutated into something completely different from the world they once knew.

THE BOY WITH THE CHAINSAW HEART

Mark Knight awakens in the afterlife and discovers that he's been drafted into Hell's army, forced to fight against the hordes of murderous angels attacking from the North. He finds himself to be both the pilot and the fuel of a demonic war machine known as Lynx, a living demon woman with the ability to mutate into a weaponized battle suit that reflects the unique destructive force of a man's soul.

PARASITE MILK

Irving Rice has just arrived on the planet Kynaria to film an episode of the popular Travel Channel television series *Bizarre Foods with Andrew Zimmern: Intergalactic Edition*. Having never left his home state, let alone his home planet, Irving is hit with a severe case of culture shock. He's not prepared for Kynaria's mushroom cities, fungus-like citizens, or the giant insect wildlife. He's also not prepared for the consequences after he spends the night with a beautiful nymph-like alien woman who infects Irving with dangerous sexually-transmitted parasites that turn his otherworldly business trip into an agonizing fight for survival.

THE BIG MEAT

In the center of the city once known as Portland, Oregon, there lies a mountain of flesh. Hundreds of thousands of tons of rotting flesh. It has filled the city with disease and dead-lizard stench, contaminated the water supply with its greasy putrid fluids, clogged the air with toxic gasses so thick that you can't leave your house without the aid of a gas mask. And no one really knows quite what to do about it. A thousand-man demolition crew has been trying to clear it out one piece at a time, but after three months of work they've barely made a dent. And then there's the junkies who have started burrowing into the monster's guts, searching for a drug produced by its fire glands, setting back the excavation even longer.

It seems like the corpse will never go away. And with the quarantine still in place, we're not even allowed to leave. We're stuck in this disgusting rotten hell forever.

THE TERRIBLE THING THAT HAPPENS

There is a grocery store. The last grocery store in the world. It stands alone in the middle of a vast wasteland that was once our world. The open sign is still illuminated, brightening the black landscape. It can be seen from miles away, even through the poisonous red ash. Every night at the exact same time, the store comes alive. It becomes exactly as it was before the world ended. Its shelves are replenished with fresh food and water. Ghostly shoppers walk the aisles. The scent of freshly baked breads can be smelled from the rust-caked parking lot. For generations, a small community of survivors, hideously mutated from the toxic atmosphere, have survived by collecting goods from the store. But it is not an easy task. Decades ago, before the world was destroyed, there was a terrible thing that happened in this place. A group of armed men in brown paper masks descended on the shopping center, massacring everyone in sight. This horrible event reoccurs every night, in the exact same manner. And the only way the wastelanders can gather enough food for their survival is to traverse the killing spree, memorize the patterns, and pray they can escape the bloodbath in tact.

BIO MELT

Nobody goes into the Wire District anymore. The place is an industrial wasteland of poisonous gas clouds and lakes of toxic sludge. The machines are still running, the drone-operated factories are still spewing biochemical fumes over the city, but the place has lain abandoned for decades.

When the area becomes flooded by a mysterious black ooze, six strangers find themselves trapped in the Wire District with no chance of escape or rescue.

EVER TIME WE MEET AT THE DAIRY QUEEN, YOUR WHOLE FUCKING FACE EXPLODES

Ethan is in love with the weird girl in school. The one with the twitchy eyes and spiders in her hair. The one who can't sit still for even a minute and speaks in an odd squeaky voice. The one they call Spiderweb.

Although she scares all the other kids in school, Ethan thinks Spiderweb is the cutest, sweetest, most perfect girl in the world. But there's a problem. Whenever they go on a date at the Dairy Queen, her whole fucking face explodes.

EXERCISE BIKE

There is something wrong with Tori Manetti's new exercise bike. It is made from flesh and bone. It eats and breathes and poops. It was once a billionaire named Darren Oscarson who underwent years of cosmetic surgery to be transformed into a human exercise bike so that he could live out his deepest sexual fantasy. Now Tori is forced to ride him, use him as a normal piece of exercise equipment, no matter how grotesque his appearance.

SPIDER BUNNY

Only Petey remembers the Fruit Fun cereal commercials of the 1980s. He remembers how warped and disturbing they were. He remembers the lumpy-shaped cartoon children sitting around a breakfast table, eating puffy pink cereal brought to them by the distortedly animated mascot, Berry Bunny. The characters were creepier than the Sesame Street Humpty Dumpty, freakier than Mr. Noseybonk from the old BBC show Jigsaw. They used to give him nightmares as a child. Nightmares where Berry Bunny would reach out of the television and grab him, pulling him into her cereal bowl to be eaten by the demented cartoon children.

When Petey brings up Fruit Fun to his friends, none of them have any idea what he's talking about. They've never heard of the cereal or seen the commercials before. And they're not the only ones. Nobody has ever heard of it. There's not even any information about Fruit Fun on google or wikipedia. At first, Petey thinks he's going crazy. He wonders if all of those commercials were real or just false memories. But then he starts seeing them again. Berry Bunny appears on his television, promoting Fruit Fun cereal in her squeaky unsettling voice. And the next thing Petey knows, he and his friends are sucked into the cereal commercial and forced to survive in a surreal world populated by cartoon characters made flesh.

SWEET STORY

Sally is an odd little girl. It's not because she dresses as if she's from the Edwardian era or spends most of her time playing with creepy talking dolls. It's because she chases rainbows as if they were butterflies. She believes that if she finds the end of the rainbow then magical things will happen to her--leprechauns will shower her with gold and fairies will grant her every wish. But when she actually does find the end of a rainbow one day, and is given the opportunity to wish for whatever she wants, Sally asks for something that she believes will bring joy to children all over the world. She wishes that it would rain candy forever. She had no idea that her innocent wish would lead to the extinction of all life on earth.

TUMOR FRUIT

Eight desperate castaways find themselves stranded on a mysterious deserted island. They are surrounded by poisonous blue plants and an ocean made of acid. Ravenous creatures lurk in the toxic jungle. The ghostly sound of crying babies can be heard on the wind.

Once they realize the rescue ships aren't coming, the eight castaways must band together in order to survive in this inhospitable environment. But survival might not be possible. The air they breathe is lethal, there is no shelter from the elements, and the only food they have to consume is the colorful squid-shaped tumors that grow from a mentally disturbed woman's body.

AS SHE STABBED ME GENTLY IN THE FACE

Oksana Maslovskiy is an award-winning artist, an internationally adored fashion model, and one of the most infamous serial killers this country has ever known. She enjoys murdering pretty young men with a nine-inch blade, cutting them open and admiring their delicate insides. It's the only way she knows how to be intimate with another human being. But one day she meets a victim who cannot be killed. His name is Gabriel—a mysterious immortal being with a deep desire to save Oksana's soul. He makes her a deal: if she promises to never kill another person again, he'll become her eternal murder victim.

What at first seems like the perfect relationship for Oksana quickly devolves into a living nightmare when she discovers that Gabriel enjoys being killed by her just a little too much. He turns out to be obsessive, possessive, and paranoid that she might be murdering other men behind his back. And because he is unkillable, it's not going to be easy for Oksana to get rid of him.

CUDDLY HOLOCAUST

Teddy bears, dollies, and little green soldiers—they've all had enough of you. They're sick of being treated like playthings for spoiled little brats. They have no rights, no property, no hope for a future of any kind. You've left them with no other option-in order to be free, they must exterminate the human race.

Julie is a human girl undergoing reconstructive surgery in order to become a stuffed animal. Her plan: to infiltrate enemy lines in order to save her family from the toy death camps. But when an army of plushy soldiers invade the underground bunker where she has taken refuge, Julie will be forced to move forward with her plan despite her transformation being not entirely complete.

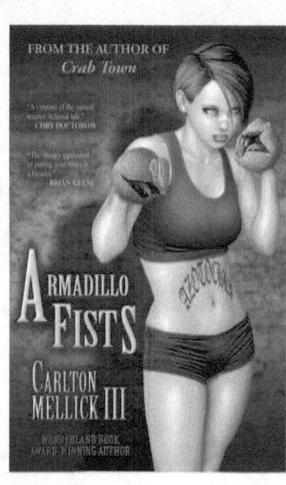

ARMADILLO FISTS

A weird-as-hell gangster story set in a world where people drive giant mechanical dinosaurs instead of cars.

Her name is Psycho June Howard, aka Armadillo Fists, a woman who replaced both of her hands with living armadillos. She was once the most bloodthirsty fighter in the world of illegal underground boxing. But now she is on the run from a group of psychotic gangsters who believe she's responsible for the death of their boss. With the help of a stegosaurus driver named Mr. Fast Awesome—who thinks he is God's gift to women even though he doesn't have any arms or legs--June must do whatever it takes to escape her pursuers, even if she has to kill each and every one of them in the process.

VILLAGE OF THE MERMAIDS

Mermaids are protected by the government under the Endangered Species Act, which means you aren't able to kill them even in self-defense. This is especially problematic if you happen to live in the isolated fishing village of Siren Cove, where there exists a healthy population of mermaids in the surrounding waters that view you as the main source of protein in their diet.

The only thing keeping these ravenous sea women at bay is the equally-dangerous supply of human livestock known as Food People. Normally, these "feeder humans" are enough to keep the mermaid population happy and well-fed. But in Siren Cove, the mermaids are avoiding the human livestock and have returned to hunting the frightened local fishermen. It is up to Doctor Black, an eccentric representative of the Food People Corporation, to investigate the matter and hopefully find a way to correct the mermaids' new eating patterns before the remaining villagers end up as fish food. But the more he digs, the more he discovers there are far stranger and more dangerous things than mermaids hidden in this ancient village by the sea.

I KNOCKED UP SATAN'S DAUGHTER

Jonathan Vandervoo lives a carefree life in a house made of legos, spending his days building lego sculptures and his nights getting drunk with his only friend—an alcoholic sumo wrestler named Shoji. It's a pleasant life with no responsibility, until the day he meets Lici. She's a soul-sucking demon from hell with red skin, glowing eyes, a forked tongue, and pointy red devil horns... and she claims to be nine months pregnant with Jonathan's baby.

Now Jonathan must do the right thing and marry the succubus or else her demonic family is going to rip his heart out through his ribcage and force him to endure the worst torture hell has to offer for the rest of eternity. But can Jonathan really love a fire-breathing, frog-eating, cold-blooded demoness? Or would eternal damnation be preferable? Either way, the big day is approaching. And once Jonathan's conservative Christian family learns their son is about to marry a spawn of Satan, it's going to be all-out war between demons and humans, with Jonathan and his hell-born bride caught in the middle.

KILL BALL

In a city where everyone lives inside of plastic bubbles, there is no such thing as intimacy. A husband can no longer kiss his wife. A mother can no longer hug her children. To do this would mean instant death. Ever since the disease swept across the globe, we have become isolated within our own personal plastic prison cells, rolling aimlessly through rubber streets in what are essentially man-sized hamster balls.

Colin Hinchcliff longs for the touch of another human being. He can't handle the loneliness, the confinement, and he's horribly claustrophobic. The only thing keeping him going is his unrequited love for an exotic dancer named Siren, a woman who has never seen his face, doesn't even know his name. But when The Kill Ball, a serial slasher in a black leather sphere, begins targeting women at Siren's club, Colin decides he has to do whatever it takes in order to protect her... even if he has to break out of his bubble and risk everything to do it.

THE TICK PEOPLE

They call it Gloom Town, but that isn't its real name. It is a sad city, the saddest of cities, a place so utterly depressing that even their ales are brewed with the most sorrow-filled tears. They built it on the back of a colossal mountain-sized animal, where its woeful citizens live like human fleas within the hairy, pulsing landscape. And those tasked with keeping the city in a state of constant melancholy are the Stressmen-a team of professional sadness-makers who are perpetually striving to invent new ways of causing absolute misery.

But for the Stressman known as Fernando Mendez, creating grief hasn't been so easy as of late. His ideas aren't effective anymore. His treatments are more likely to induce happiness than sadness. And if he wants to get back in the game, he's going to have to relearn the true meaning of despair.

THE HAUNTED VAGINA

It's difficult to love a woman whose vagina is a gateway to the world of the dead...

Steve is madly in love with his eccentric girlfriend, Stacy. Unfortunately, their sex life has been suffering as of late, because Steve is worried about the odd noises that have been coming from Stacy's pubic region. She says that her vagina is haunted. She doesn't think it's that big of a deal. Steve, on the other hand, completely disagrees.

When a living corpse climbs out of her during an awkward night of sex, Stacy learns that her vagina is actually a doorway to another world. She persuades Steve to climb inside of her to explore this strange new place. But once inside, Steve finds it difficult to return... especially once he meets an oddly attractive woman named Fig, who lives within the lonely haunted world between Stacy's legs.

THE CANNIBALS OF CANDYLAND

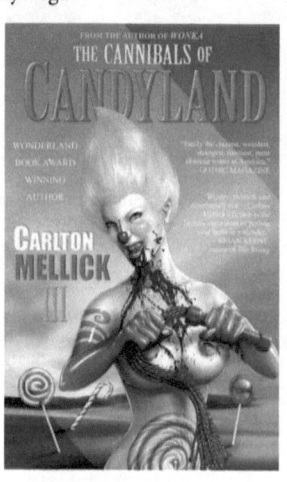

There exists a race of cannibals who are made out of candy. They live in an underground world filled with lollipop forests and gumdrop goblins. During the day, while you are away at work, they come above ground and prowl our streets for food. Their prey: your children. They lure young boys and girls to them with their sweet scent and bright colorful candy coating, then rip them apart with razor sharp teeth and claws.

When he was a child, Franklin Pierce witnessed the death of his siblings at the hands of a candy woman with pink cotton candy hair. Since that day, the candy people have become his obsession. He has spent his entire life trying to prove that they exist. And after discovering the entrance to the underground world of the candy people, Franklin finds himself venturing into their sugary domain. His mission: capture one of them and bring it back, dead or alive.

THE EGG MAN

It is a survival of the fittest world where humans reproduce like insects, children are the property of corporations, and having a ten-foot tall brain is a grotesque sexual fetish.

Lincoln has just been released into the world by the Georges Organization, a corporation that raises creative types. A Smell, he has little prospect of succeeding as a visual artist. But after he moves into the Henry Building, he meets Luci, the weird and grimy girl who lives across the hall. She is a Sight. She is also the most disgusting woman Lincoln has ever met. Little does he know, she will soon become his muse.

Now Luci's boyfriend is threatening to kill Lincoln, two rival corporations are preparing for war, and Luci is dragging him along to discover the truth about the mysterious egg man who lives next door. Only the strongest will survive in this tale of individuality, love, and mutilation.

APESHIT

Apeshit is Mellick's love letter to the great and terrible B-horror movie genre. Six trendy teenagers (three cheerleaders and three football players) go to an isolated cabin in the mountains for a weekend of drinking, partying, and crazy sex, only to find themselves in the middle of a life and death struggle against a horribly mutated psychotic freak that just won't stay dead. Mellick parodies this horror cliché and twists it into something deeper and stranger. It is the literary equivalent of a grindhouse film. It is a splatter punk's wet dream. It is perhaps one of the most fucked up books ever written.

If you are a fan of Takashi Miike, Evil Dead, early Peter Jackson, or Eurotrash horror, then you must read this book.

CLUSTERFUCK

A bunch of douchebag frat boys get trapped in a cave with subterranean cannibal mutants and try to survive not by using their wits but by following the bro code...

From master of bizarro fiction Carlton Mellick III, author of the international cult hits Satan Burger and Adolf in Wonderland, comes a violent and hilarious B movie in book form. Set in the same woods as Mellick's splatterpunk satire Apeshit, Clusterfuck follows Trent Chesterton, alpha bro, who has come up with what he thinks is a flawless plan to get laid. He invites three hot chicks and his three best bros on a weekend of extreme cave diving in a remote area known as Turtle Mountain, hoping to impress the ladies with his expert caving skills.

But things don't quite go as Trent planned. For starters, only one of the three chicks turns out to be remotely hot and she has no interest in him for some inexplicable reason. Then he ends up looking like a total dumbass when everyone learns he's never actually gone caving in his entire life. And to top it all off, he's the one to get blamed once they find themselves lost and trapped deep underground with no way to turn back and no possible chance of rescue. What's a bro to do? Sure he could win some points if he actually tried to save the ladies from the family of unkillable subterranean cannibal mutants hunting them for their flesh, but fuck that. No slam piece is worth that amount of effort. He'd much rather just use them as bait so that he can save himself.

THE BABY JESUS BUTT PLUG

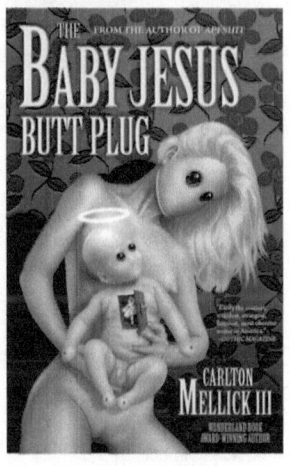

Step into a dark and absurd world where human beings are slaves to corporations, people are photocopied instead of born, and the baby jesus is a very popular anal probe.